Advanced Praise for

THE ADVENTURES OF BUBBA JONES

"The use of 'time travel' in the Great Smokies is a delightful way to interpret the area, and a method of factual presentation which captures the reader's interest most effectively. It is evident that Jeff Alt has done exhaustive research, and has presented the characters truthfully, and with respect. The family characters that Jeff Alt created show a sincere, genuine, and respectful interest in the people that they meet in time travel. I like the discussion questions that are presented. They stand to be an outstanding educational tool for teachers."

—*Joe Kelley, Great Smoky Mountains National Park ranger (ret.) and co-author of Meigs Line*

"Jeff creatively weaves a tale of discovery by integrating the cultural and natural history of the Great Smokey Mountain National Park into a family's hiking adventures. Readers are captivated as they travel through time to experience the thrill of outdoor discovery and natural history of the park along the trails, giving them the information necessary to replicate their own Great Parks adventure."

"*The Adventures of Bubba Jones* is educational and fun to read. I learned a lot."

THE ADVENTURES

of

BUBBA JONES

TIME-TRAVELING THROUGH THE GREAT SMOKY MOUNTAINS

Library of Congress Cataloging-in-Publication Data On File

For inquiries about volume orders, please contact:
Beaufort Books
27 West 20th Street, Suite 1102
New York, NY 10011
sales@beaufortbooks.com

Published in the United States by Beaufort Books
www.beaufortbooks.com

Distributed by Midpoint Trade Books
www.midpointtrade.com

Printed in the United States of America

Interior design by Jamie Kerry of Belle Étoile Studios
Cover design and illustrations by Hannah Tuohy

A NATIONAL PARK SERIES

THE ADVENTURES

of

BUBBA JONES

TIME-TRAVELING THROUGH THE GREAT SMOKY MOUNTAINS

BY JEFF ALT

BEAUFORT
BOOKS

BEAUFORT BOOKS
NEW YORK

DISCLAIMER

The Adventures of Bubba Jones is a piece of fiction. All the characters in this book are purely fictional, but the historical and scientific facts about the Great Smoky Mountain National Park are true and accurate. The maps are not true to scale. The author has spent a lifetime exploring the Great Smoky Mountains National Park and used his wealth of park facts to create this book. Many additional sources were used to verify accuracy in the creation of this adventure, listed in the bibliography.

Dedicated to Madison & William, two great adventurers.

ACKNOWLEDGEMENTS

I would like to thank the entire Beaufort Books publishing team, especially Eric Kampmann, Megan Trank, and Felicia Minerva for assembling *The Adventures of Bubba Jones* into this book and getting it into the hands of those seeking an entertaining and informative adventure. I would also like to thank the following people who were instrumental in the publication of this book: Liz Osborn; Bill Dietzer; Paul Krupin; Steve Kemp, Interpretive Products & Services Director at the Great Smoky Mountains Association; and Dana Soehn, Management Assistant/ Public Affairs at the Great Smoky Mountains National Park.

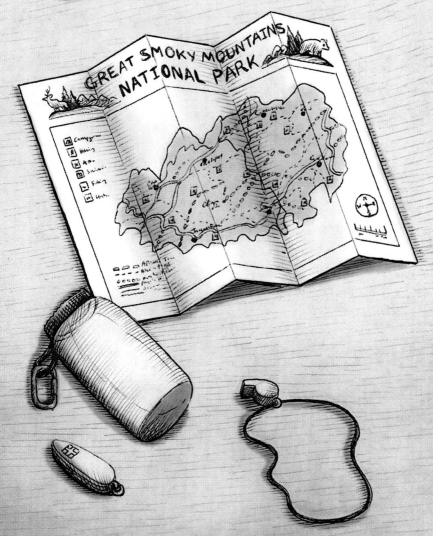

CONTENTS

CHAPTER 1

THE SECRET FAMILY LEGEND

A familiar deep voice, with an edge of excitement, startled me from my slumber in the back seat of our Jeep Cherokee.

"Hey, Bubba Jones!" (My real name is Tommy, but my nickname is Bubba Jones because of my sense of adventure.) "Wake up, we're here." It was my grandpa, Papa Lewis.

I jolted upright just in time to see the trademark national park sign announcing "Great Smoky Mountains National Park" slip by my window as our four-wheel-drive Jeep Cherokee continued deeper into the woods, leaving the domestic world behind. Seconds later, my sister Jenny, affectionately known as Hug-a-Bug for her love and compassion of everything outdoors, shouted, "Look!! A bear!"

On the opposite side of the two-lane road snaking into the park from Gatlinburg was a large black bear foraging in the trees just inches off the road, with no apparent fear of man or machinery, as if to show us who the king of the woods was. Wow! Talk about a grand entrance to our adventure, and this was only the beginning! A sense of fear and excitement gave me goose bumps all over, knowing we were going to leave the safety of our vehicle and sleep unprotected among the bears.

"Papa, are you sure it's safe to sleep outside in a tent with bears all around us?" Hug-a-Bug asked Papa Lewis.

"Don't you worry, Hug-a-Bug. Black bears are more interested in our food than us. They'd rather eat our snacks and sniff out our sweet-smelling sunscreen than eat us. We will secure those items safely away from the bears," Papa Lewis assured us confidently. Hug-a-Bug loves the outdoors, but this would be our first time ever camping in bear country. Papa's explanation seemed to put her at ease. I have to admit, I felt some relief as well!

I had been so excited the night before our adventure, I hadn't slept a wink! Instead, I lay awake imagining everything we were going to do. We had been driving since the wee hours of morning, and apparently I slept through the entire road trip. In the days leading up to our trip, time seemed to move so slowly, as if this adventure would never come. How could you not be excited about traveling to the most famous national park in the United States?! A destination with the word "great" in its name must be special! But, I was equally excited that we were accompanied by a famous adventurer; and he just so happened to be my grandpa, Papa Lewis.

Papa Lewis is named after Meriwether Lewis, and Papa's son, my dad, is named Clark after William Clark, of the famous Lewis & Clark Expedition, also known as the Corp of Discovery, commissioned under President Thomas Jefferson to explore the western United States in the early 1800's. Papa Lewis taught us that the parks and wild lands are untamed remnants from the days of Lewis and Clark, and that they allow us to escape to an earlier time, to explore, gain wisdom, exercise good health, and experience joy. Together, Papa and my dad went on many grand expeditions, and they were known as Lewis and Clark, in the spirit of the original explorers. To his credit, Papa Lewis has explored nearly every U.S. national park and wilderness since his youth, and my dad has accompanied him on quite a few of those adventures. Exploring all the parks is quite an accomplishment, but that's not quite what Papa is famous for. What I'm about to tell you is so amazing that I still can't believe it myself!

When Papa tells you about his adventures, it's not just a story; it's real! I'm not talking 3D movie real, I mean you are there in every sense of the word. You feel the fear, sweat, danger, excitement, hunger—whatever Papa Lewis experienced, you do, too. It's not just that he's a great storyteller; somehow, during his story you are transported into the adventure. When he told us about a bear charging at him, we felt the beast's hot, humid breath in our faces, our noses wrinkled at the stench of dead fish emanating from the grizzly's mouth, and our eyes widened in fear as we gazed upon the dagger-like incisors bared at us. Gathered around the dinner table one night, Papa described his encounter with a herd of buffalo in Yellowstone. Our dining table shook as if by an earthquake, rattling plates and splashing water out of our glasses, as the herd stampeded by with a deafening thunder. When Papa shared his horseback-riding adventure with the Oklahoma Cherokee Indians, we all swayed in the saddle and felt the leather of the reigns in our hands.

Describing his night at the bottom of the Grand Canyon and the star-studded velvet blanket of sky overhead, we found ourselves with outstretched hands, seeking to touch a piece of the midnight sky. When Papa Lewis sat in our living room recalling his rafting adventure down the Colorado River, we were thrust up, down, back and forth, clenching paddles in our hands, and ducking sprays of bone-chilling water. Mom thought for sure the soaked carpet in our living room was ruined, but when Papa Lewis concluded his story, everyone and everything was bone-dry, the paddles were gone, and we were all sitting dumbfounded and disoriented in our living room chairs, wondering how we came to be on dry land.

Papa Lewis looks like an outdoorsman from the 1940's. It's as if time has stood still for him. He's always wearing a button-down long sleeve oxford shirt and a pair of vintage World War II khaki parachute military pants. The cargo pocket on the right thigh of his pants is always bulging with a small rectangular object. Whatever it is in Papa's pocket, it must be pretty important and possibly classified. He never mentions it, and changes the topic if we ask him what he's carrying.

Grandma once told us, "Stop asking; one day you will know."

After each Papa Lewis story, Dad's face always splits with a grin and he says, "Why go out on an adventure when we have Papa Lewis? We don't even have to leave the house!" We love Papa's stories, but they don't keep us from our own adventures—the opposite, if anything.

Papa Lewis ends each tale by insisting that we keep his "special" storytelling ability to ourselves. He practically makes us take an oath of secrecy. Mom, Dad, my sister Hug-a-Bug, and I always assure him not to worry; we would never tell anyone. Who would believe us anyway? You would have to experience one of Papa's stories to understand and believe. Rumor has it that years ago, one of Papa's stories got so out of control, he vowed never to share his adventures in public again, so now only close family are privy to his gift. Papa is very social and loves people, but he learned early on that his unique storytelling ability can cause problems.

You see, Papa is actually able to go back in time by imagining what a place or thing was like at a given point in history. And not only does he go back in time, but he takes his listeners with him, too! Papa Lewis discovered the danger of his ability to conjure up the past as a young man on a tour with a group in Hell Creek, Montana. The interpreter leading the tour had just informed Papa's group that the first Tyrannosaurus rex (T-Rex) skeletal remains were found in that area. As Papa walked along with Grandma and several other tourists, he exclaimed aloud, "Imagine if T-Rex were alive right now!"

He had no sooner finished his sentence, than the ground split before their feet, dust and rocks spit up from the ground and a T-Rex broke free from the earth in its full terrifying size, towering over the terrorized tourists. They all shrieked and ran in panic. Thank goodness, no one was hurt. Papa and Grandma looked at each other, shocked and wide-eyed, then scattered with the rest of the group. When the local police arrived, accompanied by zookeepers with big-game hunting rifles, the ground was back to normal, as if nothing had happened. With the exception of purses, backpacks, and other personal effects strewn about by everyone who had fled in panic, nothing seemed unusual. This was before the era of closed-circuit cameras, smart phones, and video recorders, so the only proof of the incident came from personal account interviews. The FBI opened an investigation under the assumption that a theft ring might have been secretly panning for gold and created this panic as a diversion to deflect the tourists from their location. Everyone there that day who the authorities interviewed reported that they were chased out by an actual prehistoric T-Rex. After months of non-conclusive investigation, the case was closed and placed in the Unexplainable Bizarre Incidents file.

From that day forward, Papa decided to keep his talent a secret to share only with close family, preventing mass panic from happening again. Papa learned the family lesson that had been passed down through the generations going all the way back to the time of Lewis and Clark.

When Lewis and Clark returned from the Corp of Discovery Expedition in 1806 and shared stories of the wondrous wilderness they had found, our family elders had the foresight to realize that many others would soon head west, inspired by the successful Lewis and Clark Expedition. Expansion of our nation's West was great for the growth of our young country, but my family elders feared that the American wilderness would soon become overrun and many natural wonders would vanish. My ancestors decided that the family's time-traveling and storytelling abilities could serve a greater purpose. They could help preserve and protect these wild lands for future generations, so others could experience the true sense of adventure that the Corps of Discovery did. Perhaps they would not discover a new passageway to the west, but they could enjoy some of the same undeveloped wild lands that Lewis and Clark had experienced. My ancestors developed a family mission to focus their time-traveling talents to help preserve and protect America's wilderness for future generations to enjoy, experience, and utilize as needed for survival. So it went: my family took their time-travel skills and dispersed, spreading out across America with a loose-knit ideology to enjoy and preserve the great outdoors. Little did our ancestors know how precious the great outdoors would become in just a few short centuries.

After the T-Rex incident, Papa never again caused a scene or panic in public. He kept his expeditions to the confines of the US parks and wilderness, to explore and learn from the great outdoors. He learned from his grandfather that the time-travel powers he inherited were not only given to him for the purpose of exploring the great outdoors, but also to try and solve a family mystery dating back to the time of the Lewis and Clark Expedition. Even bigger than that, solving this family mystery would uncover the greatest national discovery in modern times. Unfortunately, the mystery would not be solved on Papa's watch. You see, the family mission came with a set of strict rules to hand off the time-travel skills at a given point in time based on the elder's age. The rules stated to skip a generation to preserve the family legacy as long as possible. That time had come for Papa Lewis to turn over this unsolved mystery and pass his time-travel storytelling skills to the next in line. It was time for Bubba Jones and Hug-a-Bug to take over and try to crack the mystery. This is our story. Are you ready for an adventure?

Bubba Jones, Papa Lewis, and Hug-a-Bug's Backpacking Gear List

Tent

Sleeping bag

Sleeping pad

Backpack

Cooking pot

Spoon

Mug for hot beverages

Hydration hose system and/or BPA free bottles

Water filter or treatment system

Rope, 50 feet (to hang bear bag)

First-aid kit

Pack cover

Duct tape (two feet for emergency repairs)

Compass

Map / Topography Map

Magnifying lens or glasses to read map

GPS

Whistle

Signal mirror

Water

Food (enough for three meals each day, plus snacks, and an extra day of food for emergency use)

Tooth brush

Toothpaste

hand sanitizer

Wet wipes

Biodegradable soap

Toilet paper

Bandanna

Vitamins

Head lamp/flashlight

Watch

Sealable waterproof bags (to keep gear & clothes in)

Sunscreen

Sunglasses

Bug repellent

Plastic spade shovel (for digging your cat hole)

Hiking poles

Camera

Paper/pen

Book

Repair kits

Batteries

Cell phone & charger

Park Emergency
phone number

Matches and lighter

Swiss Army knife or
multipurpose knife

Survival / lock-
ing blade knife

Stove (one burner
backpack stove)

First Aid Medicine

Clothing
(NON COTTON)

Layers of synthetics, wool,
fleece and waterproof
breathable outer shell

Dress for the weather
conditions.

Bring extra sets of clothes.

Base Layer

Underwear (2–3 pairs)

T-shirts (2–3)

Socks (2–3 pairs)

Long underwear top
and bottom (2 pairs)

Insulating Layer

Shorts

Zip off long pants/ shorts

Shirts (2–3)

Fleece jacket or pullover

Wool jacket or pull over

Outer Layer

Rain jacket or parka:
waterproof, breathable

Rain pants: water-
proof, breathable

Gaiters

Hat with rim

Hat Fleece or wool

Gloves

Boots or trail shoes
(Make sure they fit!)

Sandals or Crocs

CHAPTER 2

THE ADVENTURE BEGINS!

Papa Lewis planned our family expedition to the Great Smoky Mountains down to every last detail. This park is where his life as an adventurer began with his grandfather decades ago, and he wanted to share a special family tradition with us. He told us he wanted to pass on a legacy, but he wouldn't tell us exactly what that meant. Hug-a-Bug and I were excited and curious as to what Papa was going to share.

One thing I knew for sure: everything about the Great Smoky Mountain National Park was big. I'm talking really big. There are over 800 miles of trails, including over 70 miles of the fabled Appalachian Trail. The park is located on the Tennessee and North Carolina border, and the Appalachian Trail in the park also serves as the Tennessee and North Carolina state line, traversing the ridge line and almost evenly dividing the park in half. More than nine million people come here each year, making it the most visited US national park. The Smokies are the highest mountains east of the Mississippi River. Hug-a-Bug and I were a bit nervous to hear that the park also has the largest population of black bears in the eastern U.S. All of this is big! Now I understood why "great" is included in the park name!

The Cherokee Indians called the park home at one point in history and referred to the mist surrounding the mountains as Shaconage (shah-con-ah-jey), meaning "place of the blue smoke." Early settlers, in reference to the clouds and mist, referred to the mountains as the Smoky Mountains, and some people simply call the park the Smokies.

Papa Lewis drove our Jeep deeper into the park, weaving along a curvy two-lane road lined with thick forest. Mom rode in the front seat. Dad and Grandma Lewis were in the second-row seat, and Hug-a-Bug and I were in the third-row seat with our eyes fixated on the trees, looking for more bears. We turned off onto another road at a sign announcing Elkmont, one of the national park campgrounds. A few miles later, we rolled into the campground, a quiet, shaded area with mountain streams running through—a truly relaxing setting. Elkmont is a simple set-up with a small camp registration office, bathrooms, vending machines, and campsites.

Papa Lewis explained, "This will be our base camp for a few days."

We all stepped out of our vehicle. We pulled our gear out and worked together pitching our tents and setting up a dinning canopy.

Papa announced, "We have a big day in store for us tomorrow and we should get plenty of rest."

No one argued. We were all tired from the long drive and excitement. After we ate some sandwiches Mom had packed, we all retired to our tents for the night, just as the sun set behind a distant mountain.

The next day, everyone was up at the crack of dawn, refreshed and ready for some adventure. Sunlight trickled through the leafless gaps between trees. Birds chirped, singing their morning song. The grass dripped with beads of morning dew. Elkmont had a peaceful quietness about it, with most of the visitors still asleep in their campers and tents. Papa Lewis studied maps during breakfast. When he finished eating, he placed one foot up onto the picnic table bench and leaned in toward me and Hug-a-Bug as we scooped cereal from our bowls, hungrily shoveling spoonfuls into our mouths.

"Are you guys ready for a big day?" Papa Lewis asked.

"You bet!" I exclaimed, and Hug-a-Bug nodded eagerly with a smile.

Papa slid an unfolded topography map of the Great Smoky Mountains over to us so we could follow along as he began to explain our itinerary.

"We are here," Papa said, pointing to Elkmont on the map. He ran his finger along the Little River Trail stopping on a little triangular symbol indicating a campsite.

"We are going to campsite twenty-four," Papa Lewis said. "Your parents and grandma will meet us here tomorrow afternoon," he added, pointing to Clingmans Dome.

"Papa, it looks like Clingmans Dome is the highest mountain in the park," I observed, looking at the map.

"Yep! It's 6,643 feet above sea level. Not only is it the highest mountain in the Smokies, it's the highest mountain along the entire Appalachian Trail," Papa Lewis said, with an upswing in his voice.

"Let's go! After reliving your adventure stories at home, it'll be awesome to actually be with you on an adventure in real time! But why can't Dad, Mom, and Grandma come along?" Hug-a-Bug added.

Dad looked up at Hug-a-Bug and me with a grin, and said, "Bubba Jones, Hug-a-Bug, your Papa has looked forward to taking just the two of you on this hike for a long time. He has something special to share with you guys. We'll join you at Clingmans Dome tomorrow afternoon and spend the rest of the trip with you. So, go on, have a good time with Papa Lewis. Your gear should be all set."

"Thanks, Dad," Hug-a-Bug said.

"Look after your sister, Bubba Jones," Dad added.

"I will, Dad," I replied.

Dad, Hug-a-Bug, and I had stuffed all our backpacking provisions into our packs before we left on our trip.

I grabbed my pack and slung it over my shoulders. Hug-a-Bug and Papa Lewis did the same. Papa's pack looked like something out of a history museum. It was made out of Army green canvas. They don't even use canvas to make packs anymore. In contrast, Hug-a-Bug and I wore modern packs made out of brightly-colored, lightweight synthetic fabric. Mom and Grandma hugged us and said good-bye. Dad helped adjust our pack straps one last time and gave us each a hug, too.

"Enjoy your adventure," Dad said, standing with Mom and Grandma in our camp.

We turned towards Papa Lewis and we were just about to walk out of camp, when it happened. Papa Lewis took us on our first time-travel adventure—and believe me when I tell you, this was even more real than his living room storytelling!

Papa Lewis turned around looking at everyone, and said, "Elkmont wasn't always a relaxing national park campground. I'm going to take you back to 1906 so you can see for yourself." With that statement, Papa Lewis placed his hand on the thick book-like object bulging out of the cargo pocket on his right upper thigh and—poof!—in an instant, everything from the present vanished! We were surrounded by rows of narrow wood cabins about the width of mobile homes. Smoke billowed up from chimneys and fire pits. Our campsite—tent, vehicles, provisions, and hiking gear—was gone. Women and girls milled about in long dresses and some wore bonnets on their heads—Mom, Grandma, and Hug-a-Bug included. The men and boys, including Papa Lewis, Daddy Clark, and myself, were sporting long pants with suspenders and wide-brimmed hats, similar to photos I had seen in history books. Set off in the distance stood a post office and a railroad station. This definitely wasn't a campground—this was a little village! From the looks of the houses, it must have been quickly assembled.

For a moment we were all speechless and spellbound with amazement, with a zillion questions we were dying to ask Papa. It took me a minute to fully realize that we had just time-traveled with Papa Lewis to an earlier time in Elkmont.

Papa broke the silence, "This was one of several logging camps in the Smokies during the early 1900's. The cabins, called set-off houses, were brought in by train. That's where the loggers lived with their families."

"Nice hat, Hug-a-Bug," I said tugging on her bonnet.

Hug-a-Bug responded by snapping one of my newly acquired suspenders and said, "You look pretty dapper yourself, Bubba."

Papa Lewis turned away and began walking towards the trail before anyone could get out a single question. The rest of us continued to turn and stare in every direction with amazement. The stillness of the morning ended with a whistle from the distance. A group of men and teenage boys carrying saws and axes walked in the same direction as we were, towards the Little River, so I guess the whistle signaled the beginning of the work day. I opened and closed my eyes to see if what we were seeing was real. As fast as Papa's imagination had taken us back in time to the Elkmont logging camp, we returned to present day. The campground snapped back instantly to its modern appearance, once again sprinkled with brightly colored modern tents, shiny RVs, and campers cooking breakfast. We were wearing our modern clothes again, too.

Hug-a-Bug and I waved goodbye to Mom, Dad, and Grandma, and followed Papa down the trail. I grinned with excitement wondering what would happen next, as we walked in step with Papa Lewis.

"Papa, how did you do that?" I asked.

"If I place my hand on this pocket and imagine or mention a past event, everyone within a ten-foot radius of me will instantly time-travel back to the period I'm talking or thinking about. If I want to time-travel to a specific location, I need to be physically present at that place in the present time in order to travel there back in time."

"Way cool, Papa Lewis, but I sure was hot wearing those long pants and long-sleeve shirts in this heat," I said.

"Life was different back then, Bubba. If you grew up in the 1920's, you wouldn't have known how it felt to wear your modern-day, synthetic, lightweight clothing with wicking capability. Time-traveling really lets you experience the characters and feeling of the period. That whistle you heard came from the lumber mill in Townsend, seventeen miles away." Papa Lewis added.

As we hiked out of camp, Papa continued to feed us more information: "Time-traveling offers you the ability to answer questions, get facts, and even solve mysteries."

"Mysteries? What mysteries?" I asked.

"Well, that remains to be seen," Papa replied with a wink and a smile. And so we walked out of the Elkmont Campground on our way to our backcountry campsite.

CHAPTER 3

THE FALL OF THE GIANTS

P apa, Hug-a-Bug, and I walked along a narrow road. We passed through an asphalt parking lot and stepped around a closed gate, which blocked access to cars. The trail continued following the Little River off to our left, and the soothing white noise of the fast-moving water washed over us. The wide mountain stream roiled and frothed over many rocks and boulders. A deep sense of tranquility set in from the combination of being immersed in the shaded forest and walking along the Little River.

"This is beautiful!" Hug-a-Bug breathed.

"It is very peaceful, isn't it?" Papa Lewis commented.

A little further along the trail, we came upon a line of cabins that had fallen into ruin. They looked as if they had probably been quite inviting in their heyday. But now, doors hung half off their hinges, windows were shattered, roofs were sagging or caved in, and the elements had taken their toll on the neglected structures. One of the cottages off of the trail to the left, close to the river, looked to be recently refurbished. It was painted pink and had a river stone chimney.

"What's up with all the old run-down cottages, and why is that one house pink?" I asked Papa.

Papa explained, "This is the Elkmont historical area. The buildings are part of the Appalachian Club resort community. Back in the 1920s and 30s, before this was a park, these cottages were known as Millionaires Row. The lumber companies sold off some of the land to wealthy folks from Knoxville, who, in turn, built these summer cottages. They'd come down here to hike, hunt, fish, swim, or just to get away from the city. The pink cottage is called the Spence Cabin. It's recently been restored. It belonged to Alice Townsend, the wife of Colonel Townsend, owner of the Little River Lumber Company and Railroad. Let's backtrack out of the gate for a spell, over to the Jakes Creek Trail. I want to show you something."

We walked back out across the parking lot and down a paved car-sized path. Papa Lewis led us over to a large rustic one-storey brown sided building. It was old, but you could tell it had been restored and it looked rather livable. It had a wide porch spanning the entire length of the building. Just across the parking lot stood rows of more dilapidated small cottages.

"This was the Appalachian Clubhouse where everyone vacationing would gather for social functions," Papa said referring to the large building we stood in front of. The old cottages up the hill are refereed to as Daisy Town. A few of the Appalachian Club members and cottage owners, a Mr. and Mrs. Willis P. Davis and a Colonel David C. Chapman in particular, had the idea to make the Great Smoky Mountains a National Park, but they knew they would need a lot of help to make that happen."

"Are you saying that two people were able to convince all the private land owners to sell their land to make this a national park?"

"Not quite. What they did was help make the idea of a national park real. These folks are excellent examples of what happens when you come up with a great idea and put others before yourself. Your idea can become something bigger than you ever imagined, like the creation of the most visited national park in the United States. Whaddya say we go back and meet them?"

Papa Lewis placed his hand on his cargo pocket and said, "Let's go back to the year 1927, when the movement began to create the Great Smoky Mountains National Park."

Hug-a-Bug and I stopped in our tracks, huddled close to Papa Lewis, and braced ourselves for our second time-travel experience. In the blink of an eye, the ruined daisy town structures transformed into charming little cottages, well-kept and freshly painted. Shiny black Model T-Fords were parked in the yards. A wooden boardwalk spanned all the way through the Daisy Town cottages and led all the way up to the porch of the Appalachian Clubhouse where we stood. Our gear and clothing were transformed as well. Hug-a-Bug and I had canvas backpacks like Papa's, and we wore pants tucked into canvas gaiters, which covered our boots and shins, and laced up almost to our knees. The towering trees that had shaded us only moments ago were now mere saplings.

"What am I wearing, Papa?" Hug-a-Bug asked, looking down at her new outfit.

Papa whispered, "Talk softer, Hug-a-Bug, everyone can hear you. You're wearing the latest hiking apparel from the 1920s."

Men, in nice shirts and pants, and women, wearing long dresses and sun hats, rocked in chairs on the porch, sipping lemonade. They filled the porch, laughing, talking, playing cards and board games.

Three people were seated at a table near the porch steps in front of us and another man was standing at their table, apparently in deep conversation.

"If you want my support, you should drop the national park idea and make the Great Smoky Mountains a national forest," said the man standing next to the folks that were seated. He then stormed off the porch in a bout of anger.

Just after the man stormed off the porch, a well-dressed man and woman stood up from their seats at the table. The man had short white hair and wire-rimmed glasses. He was dressed in a suit and tie. His female companion had short dark hair, and was dressed in an equally elegant dress; hardly the wardrobe of hikers. When they stood up, the other man with whom they'd been sitting stood up with them. He had bushy brown hair and glasses. He shook the couple's hands and said to the couple, "I'm with you guys, the Great Smoky Mountains should be a national park, not a national forest."

The couple turned and stepped off the porch and headed towards their car.

Papa whispered softly, "That's Mr. & Mrs. Willis P. Davis leaving now, and the man they were sitting with is Colonel David Chapman." Papa pointed discreetly and continued to whisper to us. "They were some of the many people that used their business and political connections to help create the park."

"How exactly do you create a park?" I asked.

"Well, it took a lot of people, a lot of money, and a lot of work. As you can see, some people didn't want this to become a national park," Papa whispered.

"What's the difference between a national park and a national forest?" I asked.

"There are several differences, but the main distinction is that a national park does not allow logging and hunting; whereas in a national forest you can log and hunt," Papa whispered back to us.

Mr. & Mrs. Davis waved goodbye to Colonel Chapman before turning to stroll along the Little River, nodding and smiling to us as they passed.

A man and a boy walked by, heading towards the river carrying tackle boxes and fishing rods over their shoulders.

The boy said with excitement, "I hope we catch some more trout like yesterday!"

"Wow, I could so live here," I said loudly, waving to the fishermen as they walked by.

"Where are you from?" Colonel Chapman shouted from the porch as he stepped down the steps and walked towards us.

"We're from Cincinnati. We're staying at the Wonderland Club." Papa responded as we stood near the porch steps.

Turning to us, Papa, lowered his voice and said, "The Wonderland Hotel, was near our base camp at Elkmont, and was originally built during the height of the logging boom to lodge businessmen. The logging company eventually sold the hotel to some wealthy families who then used it as part of the Appalachian Club community to house guests. Unfortunately, the structure collapsed and was beyond repair. The park contracted to remove the collapsed remnants. The historically significant artifacts were preserved and the steps and other rock features remain."

Before we could respond to Papa, the Colonel had reached us, and extended his hand for Papa to shake. "I'm Colonel David Chapman," he said. "Welcome to the Smokies!"

"I'm Lewis and these are my grandkids, Hug-a-Bug and Bubba Jones," Papa Lewis said.

"Hug-a-Bug is an interesting name," Colonel David Chapman said with a laugh. "Won't you stay and have a lemonade with me?" he asked. He led us up to the porch and poured us each a glass of freshly squeezed lemonade loaded with sugar.

"Thank you kindly," Papa Lewis said

"Yeah, thank you," Hug-a-Bug said.

"Thanks," I chimed in as I gulped down the drink.

"That's the best glass of lemonade I've ever tasted," I said.

"I'm glad you enjoyed it; there's more if you like."

I helped myself to another glass.

"I'm working with some friends to try to make this area a national park, so everyone can experience the Smokies.

Some folks would rather keep things the way they are or make it a national forest," Colonel David Chapman shared.

"Ah, so we've heard. We are very appreciative of all your efforts, sir. I know the Great Smoky Mountain National Park is going to be a big hit!" Papa Lewis said.

"The Great Smoky Mountain National Park," the colonel mused, "It sure has a nice ring to it. You all have travelled quite a distance. It must have taken a few days to get here from Cincinnati. I do hope you enjoy your Smoky Mountain visit."

"It only took us about five hours. We could have gotten here faster if Papa Lewis didn't have to slow down through the speed trap on 75," Hug-a-Bug countered.

"My Model T tops out around 45 miles per hour—you must have a fast car! And what's '75?'" the Colonel asked with a frown.

"Our Jeep can go at least ninety miles per hour, and 75 is the highway," Hug-a-Bug answered back.

The Colonel thought Hug-a-Bug was pulling his leg, because no car that he knew of could go faster than his Model T. He looked at Papa Lewis with a smile and said, "Your granddaughter has quite an imagination."

"She sure does," Papa Lewis replied. "We should get back to our hike while we still have plenty of daylight." We set down our empty glasses and stood to go.

"Sounds good. Have a great hike," the Colonel said, with a wave goodbye from the Appalachian Clubhouse porch.

When we got out of earshot, Papa stopped and said, "I probably should have told you before I took you time-traveling that you need to blend in as much as possible. We don't want to disrupt the past. That's why our clothes change to the time period we travel to. It's best not to mention things from our present."

"Got it!" I said.

"Sorry about that, Papa," Hug-a-Bug said. "It's just hard to imagine traveling at such a slow rate of speed."

"That's okay, Hug-a-Bug," Papa Lewis answered. He continued sharing his vast knowledge: "Colonel Chapman and Mr. and Mrs. Davis were pioneers in advocating for a national park. They went on to convince others to support their cause. Colonel Chapman partnered with Arno Cammerer, associate director of the National Park Service, and persuaded one of the richest men in the world, John D. Rockefeller, to donate five million dollars to help create the park."

"That's a lot of money," Hug-a-Bug said.

"It sure is, but it took a lot more than that. North Carolina and Tennessee—the two states in which the park is located—each contributed two million dollars. All in all, it took over twelve million dollars to create this park. In 1924, W.B. Townsend, the owner of the Little River Lumber Company, sold seventy-seven thousand acres of land to the National Park Service. Thousands more people donated cash or sold off their land. Highways as you know them were not yet built in 1923, Hug-a-Bug. But, one of the reasons the Great Smoky Mountains is now the most visited national park is because it's within a day's drive of the most densely populated parts of our country."

I glanced down at the date on my digital watch to see whether we had returned to the present. Yep, 2014! I looked back towards the cottages and they had lapsed back to their dilapidated state.

It's kind of eerie and amazing all at the same time to relive history, I thought, as we continued hiking along the Little River Trail.

"Papa, how did the loggers get the trees they cut down off the mountain?" I asked.

"Mostly by train, Bubba Jones. Several of the trails in the park, including the Little River Trail that we're walking on now, were once lined with railroad tracks," Papa Lewis replied. He put his hand on his cargo pocket. Hug-a-Bug and I stayed close to Papa, knowing by now that this meant we were going to time-travel again.

"Let's go back to 1903 and take a ride," Papa said.

The sound of the rushing river was suddenly drowned out by a loud whistle, the chugging of a steam engine, and the metallic clank of a train moving along the tracks.

The ground beneath our feet was replaced by the floor of The Little River Lumber Company train engine. Our hiking poles vanished and Hug-a-Bug's and my fingers were now wrapped around shovel handles instead.

The engineer controlling the throttle levers shouted, "We need more coal."

Realizing he was talking to us, we quickly dug our shovels into the pile of coal and pitched it into the fire of the engine as we chugged along the Little River. All the while, Papa Lewis stood out of the way in the corner of the engine room with a smile. The engineer looked over at us and then did a double take, apparently a bit surprised to see three of us on board. Typically, only one person—the fireman—accompanied the engineer to shovel coal. Before the engineer could question our presence, the shovel handles turned back into hiking poles and we were walking once again alongside Papa down the trail.

"Wow, this is unbelievable! I know this was our third time-travel experience today, but I still can't believe that we just rode on a train, in the past, over a hundred years ago," I said.

Hug-a-Bug was speechless, her mouth open in amazement. She looked at me and then at her hiking poles to be sure this was real.

"Bubba," Hug-a-Bug whispered to me. "Did we just ride a train in 1903?" I nodded a yes.

"Papa Lewis, why did the loggers choose the Smokies to cut trees down?" Hug-a-Bug asked.

"Before they began cutting in 1902, the forest was much different than it is today. It was untouched forest jam-packed with massive, primeval trees. Let's travel back in time to 1897, before the lumber mills had set up shop, and take a look," Papa said.

Papa Lewis placed his hand on his cargo pocket; once again we all stood together. As we traveled back to 1897, we were suddenly surrounded by humongous trees towering over us—the biggest trees I had ever seen! The trees were so thick and massive, I felt like I had shrunk to the size of an ant! All around us in every direction were trees as wide as five feet. Hug-a-Bug and I tried to wrap our arms around a chestnut tree but it was too large.

"Look around. You have American chestnut trees, tulip poplar trees, buckeye trees, basswood trees, magnolia trees, white ash trees, pine trees, and more. This is why the lumber mills moved in. These trees were so big, that an entire home could be built from just one of them," Papa Lewis said.

"Now, let's travel a few years forward to 1905, when logging was in full operation along the Little River, and see what this area looks like then," Papa said, once again clutching his cargo pocket as we stood next to him.

A few seconds later, we found ourselves still standing in the very spot where the majestic, uncut forest had just been towering over us; only now we were all squinting from the bright sunlight streaming down unimpeded. All the huge trees obliterating the sun just moments before were gone. Nothing but massive tree stumps were left, scarring the ruined earth as far as the eye could see. It was a wasteland. We heard what sounded like sawing in the distance, as well as the echo of an ax chipping away, followed by a sharp crack as a tree tilted slowly before crashing down, shaking the ground where we stood. Piles of logs lay stacked along the railroad tracks and men were hoisting logs up onto railroad cars using a crane-like machine.

"That machine they're using to load the logs onto the train? It's called a skidder," Papa said softly.

A feeling of loss came over me as I stared in horror at the mowed-down mountain, which only moments before, had been a thriving forest of magnificent trees. The loggers had completely razed this place.

"I feel like I'm in the Dr. Seuss Lorax tale," I said, thinking of one of my favorite cartoons, where a strange creature speaks for the trees because "the trees have no tongues."

"Why would you want to cut down all the trees and leave nothing?" Hug-a-Bug asked sadly.

Papa Lewis responded, "Cutting everything down is known as clear-cutting, and it was the way logging was done at the time. The logging brought jobs and money to the locals. It went on for more than thirty years."

"What stopped the logging?" I asked.

"Tourists, who rode the Little River Lumber trains into the Smokies, and locals, who saw the thick, beautiful forest turn to barren wasteland. They grew concerned that the area might be ruined forever if the loggers kept cutting the trees down. Today, all but five percent of the Smokies is forested and twenty-five percent of that is original old-growth forest. In spite of the heavy logging, the Smokies now has the largest remaining percentage of old-growth forest. One man in particular who became angry about the logging of the park was Horace Kephart. He had moved into the area and lived deep in the mountains on the North Carolina side of the park. When he saw what the loggers had done to the raw beauty, he became an outspoken advocate to create a national park because he knew national park status would not allow logging," Papa explained.

"I'm sure glad the logging stopped and this is a national park now," Hug-a-Bug said.

Papa Lewis continued, "To be fair, it wasn't just the logging that wiped out the giant trees. A fungus made its way over from Asia from imported chestnut trees, and completely devastated the American chestnut trees. It became known as chestnut blight. Not just in the

Smokies, but everywhere in the country. That fungus eliminated even more trees than the loggers."

"Wow, that's awful," I said. Hug-a-Bug stood listening to Papa, hanging onto his every word.

In a flash, we returned to the present, and were once again walking in shaded forest beneath the tree canopy. After witnessing firsthand how big and thick the original forest was, it was obvious we were hiking through secondary regrowth.

"Time-traveling to the past is way better than sitting in Mrs. Beasly's history class!" I said. "Seeing that forest firsthand was so much more powerful than looking at a picture in our history textbook."

We continued walking along the Little River for several miles. By lunchtime, we arrived at Backcountry Campsite #24, our home for the night.

CHAPTER 4

THE LEGEND UNFOLDS WITH
SPARKLES IN THE NIGHT

Hug-a-Bug and I dropped our packs, leaned them against a tree, and sat down on some rocks surrounding a fire pit. It felt good to give our feet a rest. We sat sipping water from our Nalgene bottles and watched Papa Lewis show off his outdoorsman skills. In one fell swoop, he released his pack, swung it to the ground, unfastened two straps opening up the main compartment, and pulled out a rolled-up tent. This had been his lifestyle since he was a teenager. We helped him assemble the simple two-pole tent. Then we put all of our food and other scented items (toothpaste, deodorant, Chapstick, etc) in a bag, clipped that onto a pulley cable, which ran between two trees, and hoisted it twenty feet into the air—far out of reach of a bear's paws. We gathered some water from the nearby stream and ran it through our pump filter to purify it for drinking. We cooked dinner over a one-burner hiking stove, then gathered up some firewood and placed it next to the fire ring.

Our adventure so far was the most amazing event Hug-a-Bug and I had ever experienced, but what happened next was even more unbelievable.

As the sun set behind a distant mountain, the forest began to darken. Papa Lewis insisted that we hold off on the fire, even after it was completely dark. We found out why a short while later. We began to see lightning bugs flicker all around us. Then, all of the sudden, thousands of fireflies lit up at the very same time. They stayed lit for a few seconds and then all would go completely dark. We'd seen lightning bugs before, but never lighting in synchronicity, like blinking Christmas lights. At first, we thought this had something to do with Papa Lewis and his magical ability, but Papa had never said a word or laid a hand on his pocket. This was completely amazing. How could all these fireflies light up at the very same time?

"Papa Lewis, is this really happening or are you using your special talents?" I asked.

"No, Bubba Jones, I don't have anything to do with what you're seeing. This is one of the reasons I wanted to bring you and Hug-a-Bug here. It's also one of the many reasons the Great Smoky Mountains are so special. What you're seeing is a rare species of firefly, and the scientists think the males use their light to attract females during mating season."

We were completely surrounded by the fireflies. They were lighting up and giving us a magical light show in every direction.

"Wow, this is like a fireworks show without the booms and bangs," I said, settling on a log with Hug-a-Bug.

After about an hour of watching the synchronized fire-flies, Papa Lewis lit the kindling in our fire pit and got a roaring fire going. We moved closer to the fire and Papa Lewis began to tell us more stories.

"My grandfather took me and my cousin Will to this very same campsite forty years ago," Papa said with a smile. He continued, "We're not going to time-travel tonight, but some characters will appear during my story I'm about to tell you. Don't be alarmed."

Hug-a-Bug and I squeezed together, a bit startled when a gray-haired, bearded man resembling Papa appeared next to us on the log, and two boys appeared, sitting on a log across the fire from us.

"Papa, this is kind of spooky to have people appear out of nowhere in our campsite in the middle of the woods at night," Hug-a-Bug said.

Unfazed by our visitors and Hug-a-Bug's comment, Papa continued, "I saw the synchronized fireflies forty years ago, on a night just like tonight, sitting right here with my grandpa and my cousin. I thought for sure it was part of my grandfather's magic. But it wasn't. The synchronized fireflies are the magic of the natural world. On that same night forty years ago, my grandfather, the older gentleman sitting next to you on the log, passed on his time-travel and real-life-storytelling abilities to me, the dark-haired young man sitting across from you right now. You see, this is a family tradition that goes all the way back to the time of the Lewis and Clark Expedition. Bubba Jones, tonight, if you choose to accept it, you will take over my ability to time-travel and to recreate adventures from the past. Bubba Jones, as the oldest grandchild, you will be the primary keeper of the family time-travel skill until your sister is older. But, you're a team and need to work together. You're both still very young and this is a big responsibility. It is a family tradition to hand over these powers to the oldest grandchild who is able to read and write and is ready to explore. Bubba Jones, you are that child. These powers are meant to explore our natural wild lands. My grandfather chose this park because, as you've witnessed from the synchronized fireflies, it is a magical park so full of natural wonder."

Papa Lewis paused and then continued, "Bubba Jones, Hug-a-Bug, before you accept the family tradition to become time-travelers and keepers of our legendary family secret, there is something you must know. Having the ability to travel back in time and recreate adventures has been a remarkable experience for me. But, you need to be careful, because this ability can actually be stolen from you. If you accept this responsibility, you will have to take precautions. You will have to be on your guard at all times. Your parents and I will help you with this until you're both grown adults and feel comfortable with your new abilities. I don't want you to feel pressured to accept this responsibility. If either of you choose not to be part of this, that is okay. "

An ember in the campfire popped as a log fell down into the burning red coals, breaking our trance as we hung on every word Papa Lewis said. We sat silently staring into the fire. The ghostly figures of Papa's grand-father, of Papa, and of his cousin remained next to us, staring into the fire as well. Papa stood up abruptly, breaking the spell. His movement seemed to end the real-life storytelling, and the hologram-like figures from the past vanished.

I looked up from the burning embers, and gave Papa Lewis my answer.

"I'd be honored to take over, Papa." A lump formed in my throat, making it hard to swallow. I was nervous, yet thrilled at the prospect of time-travel, and proud that Papa Lewis had chosen Hug-a-Bug and me.

"Me too! Count me in!" Hug-a-Bug said, smiling.

"I knew in my heart that you both would accept," Papa Lewis said, and while his look was serious, he had a smile on his face. He sat back down next to us on the log by the fire.

"Papa, why do you think someone would try to steal our time-travel skills?" I asked.

"If someone sees you disappear and reappear, they could follow you and time-jump with you. If this happens, they could cause a disruption to the past, which would completely change events in the future. Our ability to time-travel is very special, and if someone else ever got their hands on it, this could be a real issue. They might abuse that power. That's why we are so careful to guard our ability and to keep it within the family," Papa Lewis answered.

Papa Lewis unbuttoned his cargo pocket. As he pulled back the flap, a cloud of brilliant sparkles burst forth. He reached into the pocket and pulled out the secret contents. Ever since I can remember, Papa had always worn cargo pants with the outline of something in the pocket clearly visible, but we never knew what it was. Finally, the mysterious contents were revealed to us. Papa was holding a tattered and worn leather-bound book.

"Just what I had suspected, a book," I said.

Papa held the book out for us to see. The pages were yellowed with age, like an old newspaper, and the thick leather cover was covered with nicks and scratches. It was obvious that this book had been around for a long time. Papa Lewis handed me the book and said, "This is a very special journal. It is our family history dating back to the Revolutionary War. There are many family stories in here. It will be up to you and Hug-a-Bug to keep this journal updated for future generations as I have done for the past forty years. In forty years, you will hand it off to the next family member in line. There is also a mystery that I've been unable to figure out, and it looks like that mystery will not be solved on my watch," Papa said.

"Mystery? What kind of mystery?" I asked.

Papa took the book back from me, carefully opened it, and turned to a page marked with a red ribbon. A wrinkled and torn scrap of paper was folded and tucked into the spine of the page. Papa pulled the paper out and unfolded it. It was covered with letters in rows and columns, but half of the paper was missing, as if it had been deliberately torn exactly in half.

"I've been trying to figure this out for years. But half of the paper is missing," Papa explained, handing the torn paper to me.

"I've seen notes like this before. It's a cipher code," I said confidently. "Thomas Jefferson used something just like this during the Revolutionary War, and he also used it as a way to secretly communicate with Meriwether

Lewis during the Lewis and Clark expedition. We learned about it in school."

"What's a cipher code?" Hug-a-Bug asked.

"It's a code made up to send secret messages. Our military and spies use cypher codes all the time to send secret information. Our history teacher taught us about it," I explained.

"You mean our ancestors were spies?" Hug-a-Bug asked.

We both looked up at Papa Lewis for an answer.

"Bubba Jones, I'm impressed that you know what cipher codes are. You're right on track," Papa Lewis said. "No, we are not a family of spies. But, some of our ancestors were U.S spies. They helped the U.S. defeat the British during the Revolutionary War and then again in the War of 1812. When word got out about Lewis and Clark's successful expedition, some of our ancestors predicted that our civilized society would soon populate the newly discovered U.S. wild lands to the west. They grew concerned that without careful planning, conservation and preservation, future generations would not be able to experience the same sense of adventure as Lewis and Clark. It's in our family blood to live for adventure. Lewis and Clark had brought back samples of plant and animal life and our ancestors had the foresight to realize some of those very plants and animals could become extinct. They realized that the great outdoors is our greatest treasure. The natural world is where we get our food and water, where we discover new medicine and cures for deadly diseases. It's where we get our energy supply, and so much more. It was true then, and it's true today."

Our ancestors formed a secret family mission to help protect and conserve nature for future generations. They wanted to be sure your generation and many more to follow will have places like the Great Smoky Mountains to go for an adventure. Some of our ancestors who had unique skills, like the ability to encode and decode cipher messages, used these talents to set up a vast secret network across the country. That network exists today and you are part of it. Time-travel is a unique skill we can use not only to help with conservation, but also to rediscover lost skills, medicines, and so much more. Our time-travel skills give us the ability to learn what existed before us, and to discover lost techniques of survival that worked before our time. Our family mission is noble and most people share our conservation philosophy. The reason our family mission is a secret is so that no one tries to misuse our time-travel skills for deviant purposes."

"Whatever happened to your cousin, Papa? Could he have the other half of the paper?" I asked.

"I'm pretty sure my cousin Will lives here in the Smokies, but I haven't spoken to him since that camping trip forty years ago, and I haven't been able to track him down. With your help, maybe we can find him while we're here," Papa said hopefully.

As the fire died down, Papa Lewis poured water over the embers and we all zipped into our tent for the night.

"Papa Lewis, what will we do if a bear comes into our camp?" Hug-a-Bug asked, peering out from her sleeping bag. She was wrapped up as tight as a mummy.

"Don't worry, Hug-a-Bug, we hung anything the bears can smell on those cables, and as long as you don't have any food or anything with a scent in our tent, they will leave us alone," Papa Lewis said sleepily. Within seconds, his slow, deep breathing told us he had already fallen asleep.

Calmed by Papa's explanation, Hug-a-Bug and I snuggled into our sleeping bags and fell asleep too.

CHAPTER 5

THE ORIGINAL GREAT SMOKY MOUNTAIN INHABITANTS

We woke up to the tantalizing, smoky aroma of bacon cooking. The tent flap was unzipped, and I could see Papa sitting on a rock, stirring eggs in a pan over the stove. Hug-a-Bug and I joined Papa out by the fire pit for a mountainside breakfast.

"How did you carry eggs and bacon out here?" I asked Papa Lewis.

"I dried the bacon in my food dehydrator and the eggs are powdered; just add boiling water and voilà," Papa Lewis said. He stirred the eggs.

We sat quietly, eating breakfast and enjoying the peaceful stillness of the morning, with birds chirping and the distant sound of the bubbling stream. As I sat there, it dawned on me that I had completely forgotten about the bears since last night. Our campsite didn't show any sign of bear activity. Just like Papa Lewis had said.

Papa Lewis looked over at Hug-a-Bug and me and said, "You have a whole life of adventure ahead of you, and the Smokies are a great place to try out your new time-traveling skills."

I had no idea what to expect now that I had inherited Papa Lewis' time-travel skills. The secret family journal was no longer in Papa's cargo pants pocket; it was now in mine. We helped clean the breakfast pans, and broke camp. We stuffed our sleeping bags and sleeping pads in our backpacks, pulled the tent stakes up, slid the tent poles out of the fabric and folded them up. Papa seamlessly rolled up the tent and tucked it into his pack. He pulled out the map, reviewed our hiking plans, and we were off, heading up the mountain to Clingmans Dome. Papa said it would be a difficult hike. The trail followed a mountain stream for several miles on a continuous upgrade and then we turned onto the Goshen Prong Trail. The trail became steeper, making each step more difficult. Hug-a-Bug and I were in pretty good shape, but this was tough hiking. We stopped for a break and that's when we realized that Papa had fallen behind. A few minutes later, he caught up to us and we all sat for a while to eat a snack and chug down some water.

"You guys are doing great," Papa Lewis said. "I'm not far behind. I'm just enjoying my own pace. I'm not as agile as I used to be." Papa was still breathing hard from the hike. He wiped sweat from his brow.

After a short break, we continued on. The trail turned away from the stream and continued to ascend. As we climbed higher, we began to smell the distinct aroma of Christmas trees, emanating from the spruce trees that dotted the landscape at the higher elevations. The tree species had gradually changed the higher we climbed, and the temperature had dropped noticeably as well.

I stopped to catch my breath and commented, "I wonder if anyone ever tried to live up here on top of the mountain. I don't know if you could do it. It would be really tough to survive, especially in the winter."

Hug-a-Bug was too winded from the climb to say anything, so she just nodded in agreement as she wiped sweat from her forehead.

Papa Lewis was right behind me and heard my question. He responded, "Bubba Jones, this is a perfect opportunity to practice your time-travel skills. Why don't you take us back to 1838? You can see for yourself what it takes to survive up here."

All morning I had been dying to try out my time-travel skills to see if they actually worked, so I gladly followed Papa Lewis' request. I placed my hand on the family journal stuffed in my pocket. Hug-a-Bug and Papa Lewis stepped closer to me and I said loudly, "Let's go back to 1838."

Seconds later, our packs and hiking poles had vanished. We were now dressed in fringed deerskin clothing. Our boots were replaced with moccasins. A large boulder had shielded our arrival from view of others. A group was sitting nearby on rocks around a roaring fire. It was really cold, so we all quickly cozied up to the fire alongside dark-haired men, women and children. Some of the men had feathers woven into their long hair and others had Mohawks. Some had colored paint markings on their faces. They were speaking a language I didn't understand or recognize. Some of them were reading, but I didn't recognize the symbols on the paper. A group sitting around another fire sang chants to the beat of drums. Several men were standing guard off in the trees away from the fire circles. Some held rifles ready to fire as they looked cautiously out into the forest; others had bow and arrows.

"Papa Lewis, those look like real guns and these people have all the characteristics of Native Americans," I whispered.

Papa led us away from the fire and whispered, "Yes, Bubba Jones, we're hiding out with the Cherokee Indians high up in the Great Smoky Mountains. The president ordered the U.S. Army to remove all Cherokee from their villages—by force if necessary—and make them move twelve hundred miles west to Oklahoma. As you can imagine, the Cherokee didn't want to leave their homes, but they were completely outnumbered by the U.S. Army, so most of them went to Oklahoma. This forced migration was known as the Trail of Tears. Some of the Cherokee refused to leave their homeland. One of the most respected chiefs, Yonaguska, fled with a band of Cherokees into the mountains to hide, in the hope of staying in the area. They were joined by others that had escaped the U.S Army. We need to be careful, especially with our white skin. They don't trust outsiders right now. We need to blend in."

We went back over by the fire to keep warm. We kept to ourselves so as to go undetected. Thankfully, Hug-a-Bug made sure her blond hair was tucked underneath a turban she wore. We didn't talk so the Cherokees wouldn't hear our English. Everyone was shivering from the cold, including us. A group of men walked into camp, returning from a hunt for food. Some of them had rifles, bows, and arrows strapped over their shoulders. Others carried dead squirrels by the tail, and several men carried a lifeless white tail deer upside-down, with its legs tied onto a long thick stick. Everyone helped the hunters skin the animal and prepare the meat to cook for food. The ground was covered with snow and the tree branches were lacquered with ice. We all sat close together wrapped in blankets. Almost everyone looked lean and hungry.

Papa Lewis whispered, "Okay, Bubba, take us back to the present."

I stepped away from the fire and walked around behind a big boulder, out of view. Hug-a-Bug and Papa Lewis followed. I placed my hand on the family journal in my pocket and whispered so that the Cherokees wouldn't hear me, "Take us back to the present."

Seconds later, we were all wearing our hiking gear once again and standing on the trail.

"Holy cow, Papa, that was scary!" Hug-a-Bug exclaimed. "What if the Cherokees discovered we were not from their tribe?"

"I'm not sure, Hug-a-Bug. The Cherokee Indians just wanted to stay in their homes that were rightfully theirs and lead their lives. Our government forced them out," Papa Lewis answered.

"That's horrible. Why would our country do that?" I asked.

"Greed!" Papa Lewis answered. "The white settlers wanted the Cherokees' land, especially after learning it had gold."

"What ended up happening to the group we just visited?" I asked.

Papa Lewis answered, "Over a thousand Cherokee Indians hid from the Army, high up in the Smoky Mountains. They struggled and some died, but it paid off. Eventually, they were allowed to stay. But, the U.S Army forced them to convict and execute one of their own band members, who had killed a U.S. soldier. That was part of the deal to be able to stay. That Indian is praised as a Cherokee hero. Today, those Cherokee are now known as the Eastern Band of the Cherokee Indians. They live on a reservation on the south side of the Great Smoky Mountains National Park. The Eastern Band of the Cherokee, when pushed, proved their determination to keep what was rightfully theirs. They sacrificed everything up there on the mountain. For that, I look up to them."

Papa continued, "The rest of the Cherokee established a new home in Oklahoma. Today, they have a thriving community there."

"I'm glad we don't treat Native Americans that way anymore," Hug-a-Bug said. I nodded in agreement.

"Me too," Papa Lewis replied.

"Well, I did it! I time-traveled and returned. I can't believe that I can do this," I said.

"Bubba Jones, I'm proud of you. You did a good job with your first time-travel episode," Papa Lewis said, with a smile on his face.

"Bubba can't use those skills to turn me into a toad or anything like that, can he?" Hug-a-Bug frowned.

"Oh no, Hug-a-Bug, Bubba Jones can't turn you into a toad. He inherited some powerful skills, but they are only meant for discovery of the past and retelling events about our natural wild lands," Papa Lewis laughed.

Hug-a-Bug smiled and let out a sigh of relief.

"Sis, you wouldn't make a very good toad anyway. Toads eat bugs, you hug them," I joked back.

We continued hiking up the mountain and soon came to a trail junction with the Appalachian Trail. We had just two more miles to Clingmans Dome. We felt a jolt of adrenaline, knowing we were almost to the top. The hike had been like walking up a rollercoaster hill. We took a standing break before continuing onward.

CHAPTER 6

ONE BIG MOUNTAIN

"**W**ow, we're almost to the highest point in the park, and we walked all the way from the bottom of the mountain!" Hug-a-Bug shouted.

"Yes, at 6,643 feet above sea level, Clingmans Dome is the highest point in the park. It is also the highest mountain along the entire Appalachian Trail, which extends from Georgia to Maine," Papa Lewis said.

We walked on, following a narrow path with beautiful mountain views. We stopped at one of the views and sat down for some water and a snack.

As we all sat there taking in the view, Papa Lewis added some more trivia: "Clingmans Dome wasn't always this high; it used to be much, much higher."

"Really?" Hug a Bug questioned.

"Can we travel back and see?" I asked looking at Papa Lewis.

"You're the time-traveler now, Bubba Jones. It's your call."

"Sounds fun. What time frame should we travel to?" I asked Papa.

"Try going back 460 million years."

"Are you serious? That's a really long time ago."

"These are some very old mountains, Bubba Jones."

Hug-a-Bug and Papa Lewis stood close to me as I placed my hand on the family journal once again and said, "Let's go back 460 million years."

Seconds later, our thin jackets were replaced with thick, puffy, hooded thermal coats. Our hiking poles had vanished and our hands were insulated with thick mittens. Ice pellets smacked us on the cheeks. The wind was so cold it stung our skin.

Papa Lewis shouted over the wind whistling in our ears, "Geologists estimate that 460 million years ago, The Great Smoky Mountains were more than double the current elevation, at least fourteen thousand feet tall—possibly as high as the Himalayas."

"Wow! So we're at least twice as high as Clingmans Dome is in present day." Hug-a-Bug shouted as her teeth chattered uncontrollably between words. "C-c-c-can we g-g-g-go b-b-back to the present B-b-bubba J-j-j-jones? This is too c-c-c-cold. I'm turning into a popsicle."

We stood together shivering as I placed my hand back on the family journal and said, trying to control my chattering teeth, "T-t-t-take us b-b-back to the p-p-p-present."

Our clothes transformed back to our light parkas. The cool temperature now felt warm compared to the subzero windchill we had just experienced.

It's amazing how old the earth is, I thought, as we trudged up the mountain.

We walked on and soon began to hear voices, car engines, car doors slamming: all the sounds of a popular tourist destination. We had reached our goal—Clingmans Dome.

We stepped up from the rocky footpath into a parking lot. Hundreds of people of all ages, shapes, and sizes were walking to and from their cars towards an overlook with a viewing area. Hundreds more people were walking back down from it. This is where we were supposed to meet Dad, Mom and Grandma, but we didn't see them anywhere.

The three of us walked up the path, following hundreds of others who had cameras around their necks, were pushing strollers, or were carrying backpacks, until we reached an observation tower and stood enjoying the view. We could see for at least a hundred miles in every direction.

"Hug-a-Bug! Bubba Jones! Papa Lewis!" My dad's voice shouted from behind us on the observation tower. Mom, Dad, and Grandma were up here enjoying the view while they waited for us. We all walked together down the path. Papa Lewis led us into a little visitor center nestled along the side of the footpath that led up to the lookout. When we entered the building, the wall to the right immediately caught my attention with some facts about Clingmans Dome. I walked closer to get the facts. One of the headings, "Spruce-Fir Forest," drew my attention. We had smelled the distinct spruce scent (which reminded me of Christmas) all day on the approach to Clingmans Dome and now I discovered why I only smelled those trees at Christmas. The Red Spruce and Fraser firs only grow in certain areas over 4500 feet. They are left here from the Ice Age. When the glaciers pushed south, they brought plants and seeds down from the northern part of the continent. As the glaciers retreated and the climate warmed, the spruce-fir forest remained up here in the cool air.

Papa Lewis interrupted my attention from the poster, "Yep, Bubba Jones, if you want to see a spruce-fir forest anywhere else you need to go to northern Maine or Canada. Our hike just from Elmont to the top of this mountain allowed you to see the same kind of change in tree and other plant species that you would if you walked all the way from Georgia to Maine!"

Our conversation continued as we exited the visitor center and headed towards the parking lot: "Papa, I also read that Clingmans Dome was named after the scientist that measured the height of the mountain," I said.

"Yep, when the park was created, people that did something big, like Clingman, would have mountains and trails named after them," Papa Lewis said.

"That's so cool. A whole mountain named after you."

"How's the adventure going so far?" Dad asked us as we all walked together to our vehicle.

Hug-a-Bug and I went on for fifteen minutes telling everyone about riding the Little River Lumber train, how we met some of the original park founders at the cabins along the Little River Trail, how we saw the Cherokee Indians who had fled to the mountains during the Trail of Tears, how we went back in time to experience the amazing original height of Clingmans Dome during prehistoric times. We told them about the synchronized fireflies and how it was so unreal that we thought it had to be the work of Papa Lewis.

Then I told everyone the biggest news in a hushed tone so no one passing by would hear me, "Papa Lewis turned over his time-travel ability to me and Hug-a-Bug."

"Papa Lewis has been looking forward to this trip for a long time," Dad said.

"You got that right, Clark," Papa Lewis said, smiling. Bubba Jones and Hug-a-Bug will do a great job time-traveling and taking over our family legacy."

"Wow! You guys have accomplished an awful lot since leaving us at the Elkmont campground yesterday morning," Mom said.

"All that in less than two days; no wonder I'm so hungry!" I said.

"Don't worry, Bubba Jones, I packed a big lunch to eat," Mom said.

We followed Dad, Mom, and Grandma through the parking lot to our vehicle, and helped Dad load our packs onto the roof of the Jeep. While Dad fastened our backpacks to the roof rack with bungee cords, Mom broke out the cooler and assembled a smorgasbord of deli meat sandwiches, carrots, chips, cookies, and lemonade on the tailgate of our vehicle. Papa Lewis, Hug-a-Bug, and I went straight for the food. I've never felt so hungry!

We all watched in amazement as Hug-a-Bug ate as much as I did (two sandwiches, several handfuls of chips and three cookies). Impressive, considering I'm nearly twice her size and she normally eats half as much as me!!

We thanked Mom and Grandma for putting together a midday meal, cleaned up our mess, and piled in the Jeep. Dad steered us out of the parking lot.

CHAPTER 7

CELEBRITY SIGHTINGS AT NEWFOUND GAP

We drove for several miles along Clingmans Dome road, with plenty of stunning mountain vistas to stare at, before coming to an intersection with Newfound Gap Road. A right turn would take us twenty miles to Cherokee, North Carolina and a left turn would take us fifteen miles to Gatlinburg, TN.

"Hey, Clark, turn left and pull into the Newfound Gap viewing area," Papa Lewis said from the passenger seat.

Dad steered our Jeep left, and a few hundred yards later veered into the Newfound Gap parking lot. We found a spot to park among hundreds of other vehicles. People milled about everywhere, enjoying a stunning blue-hazed ridgeline view of endless mountains. We all stepped out of the Jeep, and for the first time I noticed how stiff and sore my muscles were from all the hiking.

"This is Newfound Gap," Papa Lewis announced.

At one end of the parking lot stood a massive two-story, half-circle monument made of stone. It looked very official—a perfect location to give an important speech.

As we walked across the parking to get a closer look, Papa Lewis explained, "This is the Rockefeller Memorial, where President Roosevelt dedicated the Great Smoky Mountain National Park, on September second, 1940."

"Is this named after the rich Rockefeller dude that Colonel Chapman talked into donating five million dollars to make this a national park?" I asked Papa Lewis.

"That's right! A donation that big deserved recognition. The monument was built on the Tennessee-North Carolina state line."

After Papa Lewis shared all these historical facts about the presidential dedication, we stood beneath the monument looking up at it with new appreciation. But it didn't look right without a president standing up there. Hug-a-Bug looked over and saw my grin.

"Are you thinking we should time-travel back to President Roosevelt's dedication?" Hug-a-Bug asked me.

"You just read my mind, Hug-a-Bug."

"Bubba Jones, I had a hunch you would want to experience the park dedication. You will need to take us to September 2nd, 1940," Papa Lewis said.

I led everyone into the tree line, out of view of all the tourists. This would be the first time Mom, Dad and Grandma would join me as I time-traveled. We all held hands to make sure we went together.

I placed my hand on the family journal sticking out of my cargo pants pocket and said, "Take us back to September 2nd, 1940."

I heard a popping sound and everything felt different. The air was a little cooler. The trees were the same kind, but they didn't look the same. We were wearing different clothes. We could hear the chatter of lots of people like we were at a busy festival. We stepped out of the trees, and everywhere we looked there were people dressed up in nice clothes from an earlier period. There must have been at least two thousand people gathered at Newfound Gap. Men and boys wore ties and suspenders. Women and girls wore long dresses and skirts. Some wore uniforms. Our family was adorned in similar clothing and we blended right in. A convoy of old-fashioned black cars was parked near us. The Rockefeller Memorial was decorated with flags. A roofed bandstand was on the left side of the memorial and a roofed shelter flanked the right side. Everyone in the parking lot was facing the memorial. Hug-a-Bug and I squeezed between the mass of people and found our way to the front row. A large circular sign with the words "Department of the Interior" and a picture of a buffalo in the center hung on the rock wall of the Rockefeller Memorial, below a podium draped with a red, white, and blue cloth. A man whom I immediately recognized as Franklin D. Roosevelt stood at the podium. Dozens of important-looking and well-dressed men and women sat in rows of chairs behind the president.

A voice crackled over a microphone, and a hush fell over the audience. You could now only hear the wind in the trees.

"Ladies and gentlemen, the president of the United States," the voice announced. The crowd erupted in claps and cheers before again falling silent. A moment later we bore witness to President Roosevelt's dedication of the opening of the Great Smoky Mountains National Park:

"Here in the Great Smokies . . . . . . we've come together to dedicate the mountains, streams and forests to the service of the American people . . . ." The president continued for several minutes, and was followed by more clapping and cheering.

Mom, Dad, Papa Lewis and Grandma found Hug-a-Bug and me in the crowd after the speech, and we all walked together back to the tree line until we were out of view. We all held hands once again, I placed my hand on the family journal, and I took us back to the present. We stepped out of the forest and saw our Jeep parked nearby, reassuring us that we were back in the present. Nobody seemed to take notice of us.

We all walked back over to the Rockefeller Memorial and climbed the steps up to where we had just witnessed President Roosevelt deliver the park dedication speech. With the president's words still fresh in our minds, Hug-a-Bug and I playfully took turns pretending to make the speech ourselves. Other tourists were standing up on the memorial with us, and we overheard a man and woman whispering back and forth on how impressed they were that we kids were able to quote parts of a presidential speech given over seventy years ago. Hug-a-Bug and I smiled, knowing they would never believe we had just heard the speech live, as Mom snapped pictures of us and posted them to her Facebook page.

As we descended the steps from the Rockefeller memorial, I noticed a sign posted along a trail at the foot of the memorial, with the heading "'Appalachian Trail" and

"Katahdin Maine 1,972.0' miles." With all the excitement of time-traveling to the park dedication, we hadn't paid attention to this sign until now. As we stood there, we caught a whiff of an awful stench, a combination of dirty socks, sweat, and body odor. Seconds later, the source of the offensive odor walked by, apparently following the Appalachian Trail. Two men with hiking poles in each hand and carrying large, heavy backpacks paused near us, looking around. It was obvious these guys had been in the woods for a while, and we changed our position to get upwind of the smell.

"Where are you going? " I asked them.

One of the hikers looked over at me and responded, "There." Lifting his hiking stick up and using it to point to 'Katahdin Maine 1,972.0' on the sign. "We're thru-hikers."

Other people overhearing the hiker's answer crowded around and began peppering them with questions and snapping pictures.

"Thru-hikers are people who walk the entire Appalachian Trail continuously from Georgia to Maine, all in one season," Papa Lewis whispered to us. "These guys have already walked over 200 miles from Springer Mountain, Georgia and they plan to continue for another 1,972 miles."

"Whoa, that's a long walk," I said.

"The Appalachian Trail, also known as the AT, is the state line between Tennessee and North Carolina in the Great Smoky Mountains National Park. The AT starts in Georgia and follows the ridge of the Appalachian Mountains through fourteen states, all the way to Maine," Papa Lewis said.

Knowing how hungry she was after just two days in the woods, Hug-a-Bug pulled out two granola bars from her pocket and asked, "You guys want some snacks?" waving her granola bars in front of the hikers. They quickly snatched the bars from Hug-a-Bug.

"Thank you! When someone does something nice and unexpected along the trail, it's called trail magic," one of the hikers told Hug-a-Bug. He tore open the wrapper and shoved half of the bar into his mouth. In two bites he ate the whole thing. Other tourists began giving the hikers more snacks.

"Every year, a few thousand hikers attempt to walk the entire trail. But, only a few hundred finish. Others walk it in smaller bits over time," Papa Lewis told us. We stood with the crowd gathered around the thru-hikers.

"Who was the first person to walk the entire trail?" I asked Papa Lewis.

"The first solo thru-hiker was Earl Shaffer in 1948. No one believed he did it because no one ever had done such a thing. He had to prove his accomplishment with photos and journal entries," Papa Lewis said.

"I would like to meet him," I said.

Hug-a-Bug, Papa Lewis, Mom, Grandma, and Dad all knew the drill, and followed me back into the tree line and out of view once again, and we huddled together.

I placed my hand on the family journal and said, "Take us back to 1948 when Earl Shaffer hiked across Newfound Gap on the Appalachian Trail."

A popping and hissing sound erupted and the forest looked slightly altered. We stepped out of the tree line and walked back to the Newfound Gap parking lot. It was obvious we had traveled back in time. We were wearing clothes similar to when the president made his dedication speech. The parking lot was filled with old-fashioned 1940s-era cars and tour buses. People milled about everywhere taking pictures and enjoying the view. We heard gears grinding as a tour bus climbed into view, up along Newfound Gap Road, from Gatlinburg. The bus turned into the Newfound Gap parking lot and came to a halt near the Appalachian Trail sign. The bus doors swung open, and a dark-haired man wearing an Army-issued canvas rucksack stepped off the bus.

"That's Earl Shaffer," Papa Lewis whispered as we stood near the bus and the trail sign.

The bus driver hollered to Earl, "Watch out for the bears and rattlesnakes and be careful."

"I'll be fine. Thanks for the ride."

They were even scared of the bears in 1948, I thought.

As Earl neared where we stood, I couldn't resist the opportunity to meet him.

"Are you Mr. Shaffer?" I asked.

"Yes I am. How did you hear about me?"

Earl's face was a deep red and his nose was blistered with sunburn.

Papa Lewis chimed in, "We heard there was a man attempting to walk the entire Appalachian Trail and you look like you've been in the woods for a while, thought you might be him."

"You found me. I just picked up groceries at Ogle's Market in Gatlinburg and caught a bus ride back to the trail. I have lots of miles to walk yet today. I better go,"

Earl replied. He shook our hands and then continued walking north on the Appalachian Trail.

"Wow! We just met the very first thru-hiker, right here in the Great Smoky Mountains," I said proudly.

"Earl Shaffer went on to become the first person to walk the entire trail. His backpack and gear are now in the Smithsonian museum," Papa Lewis told us. "The AT is marked by a white painted marking on trees or signs along the way. There are three walled lean-to shelters spaced along the trail for hikers to camp in. It takes hikers four to six months to complete a thru-hike. Thousands of hikers have completed the trail, but Earl Shaffer was the first."

"Hey Papa Lewis, who was the first female to walk the AT solo?" Hug-a-Bug asked.

"Grandma Gatewood hiked the entire trail in 1955 at the age of 67, becoming the first woman to walk the trail solo, and she walked it two more times after that."

"Bubba Jones, can we meet Grandma Gatewood please?" Hug-a-Bug asked.

"Let's do it!" I replied.

We left the parking lot and walked back to our time-travel hideout in the tree line and once again, huddled together. On my command, we time-traveled to Grandma Gatewood's 1955 thru-hike at Newfound Gap.

We stepped out from the woods and into the parking lot which was now dotted with 1950s-era cars and tour buses. The vehicles looked newer than the ones we saw when Earl Shaffer walked through, but they were still old-fashioned. We stood in the same spot along the Appalachian Trail where we had just met Earl Shaffer moments ago.

"Look over there. Here comes Grandma Gatewood," Papa Lewis said, pointing across the parking lot towards the Appalachian Trail.

We saw a gray-haired woman step out from the woods where the AT spits out onto Newfound Gap Road. She crossed the road and into the Newfound Gap parking lot and walked straight towards us. As she drew closer, we noticed that she wasn't carrying a traditional backpack. As a matter of fact, she didn't even really look like a hiker at all. She had a duffel bag perched over one shoulder. She wore a flannel shirt and long pants. She was wearing tennis shoes and she had a tree branch she was using as a hiking stick in one hand.

As Grandma Gatewood closed in on where we stood, Hug-a-Bug spoke up. "Grandma Gatewood, is that you?"

The old woman stopped and looked at Hug-a-Bug and answered, "That's what they call me."

"I'm honored to meet the first solo female thru-hiker," Hug-a-Bug said as she held out her hand to Shake Grandma Gatewood's.

Grandma Gatewood stopped and shook Hug-a-Bug's hand.

"How come you're not carrying a backpack or wearing hiking boots?" Hug-a-Bug asked.

"That stuff's for wimps. You don't need it," Grandma Gatewood answered.

Grandma Gatewood continued, "I suppose you heard I sleep under a shower curtain too? Well, it's true. Who needs a tent?"

Then Grandma Gatewood smiled at Hug-a-Bug and continued along the trail.

As she walked out of sight, Papa Lewis gave us some more facts. "Grandma Gatewood was sixty-seven and had twenty-three grandchildren when she hiked the trail. Some people were concerned for her safety when they met her along her journey. But she did it. She completed the whole journey. At the time, only five men had completed solo thru-hikes—no women."

We stepped back into the trees once again and traveled back to the present. The two present-day thru-hikers had resumed their hike, leaving behind the group of tourists that had encircled them. We all watched them walk further down the AT, just as Earl Shaffer and Grandma Gatewood had before them.

"That sure is cool how one man took this long walk on the AT and how so many others have followed in his footsteps," I said. We watched the thru-hikers until they faded out of sight down the trail.

Hug-a-Bug proclaimed, "I want to hike the Appalachian Trail someday. But, I think I want more than a shower curtain to sleep under."

"We will make sure to hike on the AT while we're here," Papa Lewis answered.

Hug-a-Bug smiled . "Awesome!"

"Many people experience the AT for the first time right here in the Smokies. The AT continues in the park for over seventy miles. But, that's not the only trail here. There are over eight hundred miles of trails in this park," Papa Lewis explained.

"Come on, let's go explore another area of the park," Dad said as he led the way back to our Jeep.

CHAPTER 8

THE OTHER SIDE OF THE MOUNTAIN

hen we got into the Jeep, Dad gave us a run-down of the next leg of our adventure: "While you were hiking, we moved our basecamp to the Cataloochee campground, on the southeast side of the park," Dad said. He downshifted the Jeep to keep us from going too fast on the steep downgrade heading towards Cherokee, North Carolina. "And I have some exciting news! My brother and his family are driving up from Atlanta, and they are going to join us for the rest of our Smoky Mountain adventure!"

"Awesome! We get to spend time with Uncle Boone, Aunt Walks-a-Lot, and Cousin Crockett!" Hug-a-Bug shouted.

You see, our extended families all have nicknames, too, based on each one's unique love of adventure and exploring—trail names, I guess you could call them. Uncle Boone's real name is Jack and his trail name is in the spirit of the famous frontiersman, Daniel Boone. Aunt Walks-a-Lot's real name is Terry and she earned her nickname because she loves to hike. Cousin Crockett's real name is Anthony and his trail name comes from the famous Davy Crockett.

"Why didn't you tell us they were coming before, Dad?" I asked.

"We invited them, but they weren't sure they'd be able to make it. Boone just let me know yesterday, while you guys were out hiking. I wanted to make sure they were coming before I said anything—this way it's a nice surprise for you!"

Uncle Boone's family lives so far from us that we hardly ever get to see them. The Great Smoky Mountain National Park is the halfway point between our home and theirs, and we have always wanted it to be our family meeting place. Now it was finally happening! I couldn't wait to see Crocket—he's a year younger than me and two years older than Hug-a-Bug. The three of us were playmates as toddlers until he moved away. Thinking back, I remembered that he had had trouble learning to walk—his left leg hadn't seemed to work right.

"Hey Dad, did Crockett ever learn to walk?" I asked.

"Your Uncle Boone and Aunt Walks-a-Lot have taken Crockett to lots of doctors and therapists over the years, and I understand that he is walking now."

As we drove, I rifled through the family journal and pulled out the torn sheet of paper with the cipher code on it. Not knowing the secret message felt like unfinished business.

"I sure would like to find the rest of this code," I said, studying it in the backseat with Hug-a-Bug. "We should try and find your long-lost cousin while we're here, too, Papa Lewis."

"That would be nice, Bubba Jones. I just don't know where to begin. It has been so long since we've seen each other—forty years to be exact."

After a short while, we made it through the last of the steep switchbacks, and we pulled off of Newfound Gap Road onto the Blue Ridge Parkway, a separate national park entity that skirted the southeastern perimeter of the Great Smoky Mountains National Park. We continued on through the Cherokee Indian Reservation and onto several other rural two-lane roads before re-entering the Great Smoky Mountains National Park. We drove slowly up a steep gravel road until we reached the top of a mountain, and then coasted down into a beautiful cove with grassy meadows, older frame buildings, and lush mountain views. We saw a sign announcing Cataloochee campground, and pulled in.

"Are we going off the grid or what?" I asked.

Papa Lewis smiled and answered, "There is something very special in this area of the park that you have to see."

We walked through the campground and I immediately recognized our bright orange tent standing out from the shaded green woods. After our hike with Papa Lewis, it was nice to be back at camp with a cooler full of food. Even though we had had a big lunch, I was hungry again and looking forward to digging in. As we parked the Jeep, we saw familiar faces in the campsite next to us—Uncle Boone, Aunt Walks-a-Lot, and Crockett had arrived and were busy setting up camp. They had set up their tent and they were filling it with bedrolls and sleeping bags.

We jumped out of the Jeep, excited to see our long-distance relatives. For the next half hour, there was hugging, smooching, and happy words—all the celebrating that goes with a reunion.

It was a little strange seeing Crockett after all these years. Heck, Hug-a-Bug had still been in diapers when he moved away, and although Crockett had been three years old at the time, he hadn't yet learned to walk. We noticed, now, however, that he was sporting a metal brace on his left leg, from the knee down. And while he walked with a limp and a bit of a stiff gait, he was getting around quite well. I hoped he would be able to hike with us.

As one of Papa Lewis' sons, Uncle Boone knew all about the family time-travel secret, as did the rest of his clan, so we shared how I inherited the time-travel skills from Papa Lewis. I told our extended family about how we traveled back in time to the beginning of the national park, how we camped with the Cherokee hiding up in the mountains during the Trail of Tears, how we heard Franklin Delano Roosevelt's park dedication speech, and how we met the two legendary Appalachian Trail hikers, Earl Schafer and Grandma Gatewood. Then I took the family journal out of my cargo pocket and showed Crockett the torn paper bearing half of the cipher code.

"Wow! We need to figure that message out," Crocket said.

"I know, right? We also need to help Papa Lewis find his cousin," I said. "Papa Lewis took Hug-a-Bug and me to the same spot where he inherited his time-travel skills from his grandfather, our great-grandfather. Papa Lewis was with his cousin Will when he camped there forty years ago. He hasn't seen his cousin since that adventure. When Papa told us about them, we could actually see them sitting with us around the fire! They were like holograms. That's where Papa Lewis handed over the family journal and time-travel skills to me," I explained.

"Wow! That's so cool, Bubba Jones," Crockett said.

"Yeah, I didn't see that coming. And it's been an amazing ride, to actually *see* history as it *becomes* history!"

Our growling stomachs reminded us that it was time for dinner. Everyone worked together to assemble a big feast. Crockett, Hug-a-Bug, and I gathered firewood and placed it in the fire pit. Uncle Boone and Dad burned some tinder beneath the logs and stoked up a nice fire. Papa Lewis set up a spit over the fire and began to slow-cook some chicken. Meanwhile, Mom, Aunt Walks-a-Lot, and Grandma whipped up a salad, baked beans, coleslaw, and lemonade. It was a perfect evening to eat outside, and we all gathered around the picnic table. Per Hug-a-Bug's request, we capped off our meal with s'mores. Hug-a-Bug assembled rows of graham crackers and pieces of chocolate along the edge of the picnic table, while Crockett and I toasted marshmallows on skewers. We kept the assembly line of s'more sandwiches going until everyone got their fill.

CHAPTER 9

A BIG SURPRISE

O ur usual tradition after a family meal is for Papa Lewis to recount an adventure and bring it back to life. But now, we were actually on an adventure with him.

As the sun dropped behind distant mountains and reminded us that dusk was upon us, Papa Lewis insisted that we take an evening stroll with him to see something special. We all followed him out of the campground and onto a gravel lane with a view of a lush green meadow. The far reaches of the meadow were encased by a thick forest wall that continued over mountains for as far as the eye could see.

"This is Cataloochee Valley," Papa Lewis said.

Scattered throughout the field, grazing in the grass, were dozens of animals that looked kind of like deer, but bigger. Their fur was short like a deer's but the color was more of a marbled brown and tan. Some of them were wearing collars.

"These are elk. Elk are the second largest of the deer family—moose are the largest. The ones with large antlers are the males, or bulls. They can weigh over half a ton! The males grow large antlers in the spring and lose them in the winter. The smaller elk are females, or cows, and the little ones are calves," Papa Lewis explained

"They seem so at peace here," Uncle Boone said. We stood along the road, snapping pictures and filming video.

"Why are the elk only in this part of the Smokies?" Hug a Bug asked.

"Elk were once abundant throughout the Great Smoky Mountains and surrounding region, but over-hunting killed them all off hundreds of years ago. This is a small herd that was brought here by the national park to rein-troduce them to the area. The park is tracking them with radio collars. The herd has grown, and it's been a huge success. It will take time for the elk to populate the rest of the park," Papa Lewis said.

"Hey Bubba Jones, let's go back to when the elk were thriving in the park," Crocket said, excited to time-travel with us.

"We can do that."

Papa Lewis suggested we go back three hundred years in time to get a good feel for these animals which once roamed the park in huge numbers. I led everyone into the tree line, out of view of some other visitors watching the elk. We huddled together, forming a circle.

I placed my hand on the family journal and said, "Take us back three hundred years."

We all stepped out of the tree line and were surprised at what we saw. The elk were grazing in the field in larger numbers, but so was a small herd of buffalo. Before any-one spoke up to ask Papa Lewis what was going on, a black bear charged out of the trees towards a small elk calf. The rest of the herd bounded away from the approaching bear. The baby elk didn't have a chance against the bear; the bear brought it down and set to devouring it in a matter of minutes. The whole scene made me uneasy. Everyone else must have felt the same way because not a word was said as all of us started walking back to the tree line, anxious to return to the present. Just before I placed my hand on the journal, the air was pierced by the high-pitched scream of a distant mountain lion. The sound sent a chill up my spine.

I placed my hand on the family journal and said, "Take us back to the present."

We stepped out of the tree line and cautiously looked around for any signs of mountain lions or buffalo. The buffalo were gone and we didn't hear any mountain lion screams, which assured us that we were back in the present.

"That was awesome," Crocket said.

"You wouldn't think it was awesome if you were that poor baby elk," Hug-a-Bug said.

"That was hard to watch, but that's the way things work in the wild," Papa Lewis said.

"Papa Lewis, where did the buffalo come from?" I queried.

"Was that a mountain lion we heard?" Hug-a-Bug asked.

"Buffalo, mountain lions, and red wolves all once called the Great Smoky Mountains home, along with the elk. Even though the elk are back in the park, this area isn't quite as wild as it once was. The elk reintroduction is a huge step towards that. The mountain lions were natural predators of the elk and buffalo. For now, the elk in the Smokies don't have that threat. But, as you witnessed, the black bear prey on the younger elk. The park has plenty of other carnivorous hunters like the bobcat and coyote, but those are smaller animals and don't pose a threat to the elk," Papa Lewis informed us.

We all walked back to our camp, and Uncle Boone put a few logs on the fire. We sat up talking about the elk, buffalo, bear, and mountain lions until the logs burned down to embers and we all decided to call it a night. I think I fell asleep as soon as my head hit the pillow. I was so exhausted from the action-packed last few days.

At some point in the night, a high-pitched, screeching bugle sound followed by a series of grunts woke me up. I sat straight up and looked around, but it was still dark out, and I couldn't see anything. I lay back down, tense and listening. Then, I heard it again. It was definitely an animal, and it sounded big.

"What is that?" Hug-a-Bug whispered, sitting up in her sleeping bag.

"That's an elk call. The bulls make that sound frequently in the fall during rutting, but it's not uncommon for the younger elk to bugle throughout the year," Papa Lewis said.

After hearing Papa Lewis' explanation, Hug-a-Bug and I relaxed and faded back to sleep.

I woke up to the damp earthy smell of morning as I lay in my sleeping bag, watching the sun's bold, red-orange glow slowly rise over a distant mountain. It must have rained during the night. Grandma and Papa Lewis were already up, sitting by the fire pit. I crept quietly out of the tent so as not to wake the others.

Papa Lewis whispered, "Good morning, Bubba Jones," and Grandma gave me a bear hug before handing me a mug of hot cocoa.

"Ah, hot chocolate and family, what more could you ask for?" I sighed.

Papa Lewis motioned for me to follow him, and we quietly walked out of camp and back over to the Cataloochee Valley where we were once again treated to the sight of several beautiful elk grazing in the grassy field. After a short while we walked back to camp.

As we entered back into our campsite, I noticed there was a lot more movement. Mom, Dad, Hug-a-Bug, Uncle Boone, Aunt Walks-a-Lot, and Crocket had all emerged from the tent, dressed and ready for adventure. This would be the first full day with our extended family in the Smokies. It had rained overnight, but the sun and blue sky were all we could see now. Dad and Mom had said the night before that they would make breakfast for everyone, and they were now busy opening coolers and setting up cooking equipment.

"Hey Clark, I'll take my eggs over easy," Uncle Boone said to Dad, who was standing at the end of the picnic table, manning two skillets filled with eggs and bacon, over the burners of our propane stove. Everyone around the table put in their egg orders to Dad, while Mom brewed up some coffee and cut up some fresh fruit.

"Papa Lewis, who lives in the houses we saw out there near the elk?" Hug-a-Bug asked.

"I wondered the same thing—it's so peaceful here, I figured others besides the Cherokees must have lived here at some point, before the Great Smoky Mountains became a national park," I said.

"We haven't really talked much about the settlers that called the Smokies home, have we? No one but park personnel live in this valley now," Papa Lewis answered. "You probably thought those homes were still occupied because they are frame houses similar to what you see in the present day. This valley and several other areas of the Great Smoky Mountains were home to many white settlers even when the Cherokee Indians still lived in the area. The Smokies had entire communities that thrived before the park was created. Even then, some settlers continued living within the national park boundary under various agreements with the park service. In 1910, there were around 1,200 people living in the Cataloochee Valley. Some of the homes, barns, and churches that you saw have been preserved. We're going to travel to Cades Cove today, and you will get a good sense of what life was like back then in the Great Smoky Mountains."

"On the way, do you mind if we stop at the Cherokee Indian Village?" Dad asked as he scraped the remaining eggs and bacon onto his own plate and sat down to eat.

"That sounds good," Uncle Boone responded.

"I would like to hike Mt. Le Conte before the end of the trip," Aunt Walks-a-Lot said.

"Can we stop at the Oconaluftee Park Visitor Center? There are a few things in my Junior Ranger book that I need to do," Hug-a-Bug asked. Hug-a-Bug had picked up a Junior Ranger booklet at Sugarlands Visitor Center when we entered the park.

"We will have plenty of time to do all that before we leave the Smokies," Dad responded.

"Hey Bubba Jones, can you show me that torn coded letter again?" Crockett asked.

"Sure. Why?" I responded.

"I'd really like to help solve the mystery," Crocket replied.

"Let's ride together and look at it on the way to the Cherokee Indian Village," I answered.

After breakfast, everyone worked together as a team, and it took less than an hour to take down our tents, break camp, and get on the road headed back towards Cherokee. Crocket and I rode with Uncle Boone and Aunt Walks-a-Lot. Our convoy crept out of the Cataloochee Valley, over a tall mountain. For the next thirty-nine miles, we backtracked along the same roads we had taken to get to Cataloochee. As I sat in the backseat, swaying with the switchback turns, I couldn't help but think about our adventure so far and my new time-travel ability. To be able to go back to any point in history and then snap back to the present was pretty cool!

CHAPTER 10

As Real as it Gets

I pulled out the coded piece of paper from the family journal and handed it to Crockett.

"You know what the code looks like to me? A cipher code, like what Thomas Jefferson used with Lewis and Clark," I said. Crocket held the torn paper in his hands and slowly examined it.

"I think you're right, Bubba Jones, but why would our family send secret codes?"

I explained to Crockett what Papa Lewis had said about how some of our early ancestors were masters of coded messages during the Revolutionary War and the War of 1812.

"But what's so secret that they had to write a coded message?"

"I'm not sure."

"Before we can even try to decipher the message, we need to find the missing half."

"Yep, you're right. I think if we locate Papa Lewis's cousin, Will, he might know something about the missing piece."

"Do you think it's possible Will has the missing half?"

"Let's hope so. If Will still lives in the area, it would be worth checking into. But, Papa Lewis said he checked and couldn't find a phone number for him in any of the counties around the park. "

"Can I see the coded letter?" Aunt Walks-a-Lot asked.

Crockett handed it up to her from the backseat. After a few minutes she handed it back to me and said, "I wouldn't know the first thing about how to read that, let alone finding the missing half. Good luck!"

We passed a sign announcing "Cherokee" and another sign directing traffic to "Oconaluftee Village." We followed Mom, Dad, Papa Lewis, Grandma, and Hug-a-Bug's vehicle into a parking lot for the Oconaluftee Village.

We all emerged from our vehicles and Papa Lewis shouted, "Hey Clark, bring back memories?"

"It sure does."

Mom and Dad had stopped for a night in Cherokee on their honeymoon and toured the village, and were excited to be back for another visit. We stood in line for tickets among hundreds of others, eager to learn about the Cherokee Indian culture. The village is a re-creation of a Cherokee Village in the late 1760s, a time before the Cherokee were forced to leave the Great Smoky Mountains on the Trail of Tears. As soon as we stepped into the village, I felt like I had entered another time period even though my hand had never touched the family journal. At first I thought Papa Lewis was playing some sort of trick on me. We were immersed in an actual village. Real Cherokee Indians wearing traditional clothing busied themselves in the tree-shaded village, going about everyday life in the 1760s . But, they were actually present-day re-enactors demonstrating how their tribe once lived. There were small, one-room log cabin homes. We watched two Indians burning out a large tulip poplar log, to make it into a canoe. Some teenage boys were playing the Cherokee version of stick ball. The village had a sweat lodge, a log-lined cavern that people used to clean themselves of impurities. Several Cherokee women were making pottery. A young man dressed in authentic buckskin, like what we had seen up in the mountains when we time-traveled to the Cherokee hideout, was busy making arrows and spears. The entire village was animated. It was amazing!

I learned that the Cherokee were one of the most civilized Indian tribes. They had their own written language and they even published a newspaper. Hug-a-Bug, Crocket, and I lost track of our parents and grandparents as we strolled through the village. I didn't feel the need to time-travel with all the re-enactors bringing the past to life for us. We walked past the council meeting building, a large, round-roofed hut where tribal meetings and ceremonies were held. The three of us ducked in to have a look. The log structure had a high ceiling with a hole in the center for smoke from the fire to escape. The walls were lined with rows of wood benches arranged like bleachers to hold large numbers of the tribe. No one was in the council building when we stepped in. We sat down on one of the benches.

"Let's have our own council meeting. We need to come up with a plan to find Papa's cousin, Will," I said. "Papa already checked the local phone books and came up with nothing."

"What about checking with the park rangers?" Hug-a-Bug suggested.

"How would they know about Papa's cousin?"

"Maybe Papa's cousin worked for the park."

"We could also check the courthouse records in the surrounding towns for property deeds and marriage license records," Crockett said.

"These are great ideas. I think we have a good start," I replied.

Some other visitors stepped into the council meeting building, which prompted us to end our meeting. We stepped out of the structure and walked around until we found Uncle Boone, Aunt Walks-a-Lot, Papa Lewis, Grandma, Mom, and Dad talking with a re-enactor dressed as a fur trader. He was explaining how the Cherokees traded animal pelts with the white settlers in exchange for munitions and other domestic items. After the re-enactor finished, everyone was ready to move on to our next adventure. We left the village, and when we got into the parking lot, we huddled together in a circle to discuss our plans. We agreed to grab some lunch and then stop at the Oconaluftee Park Visitor Center. Little did we know that we were about to stumble upon a breakthrough with our family mystery!

CHAPTER 11

THE WILD GOOSE CHASE

The Oconaluftee Visitor Center is located off of Newfound Gap Road, as you enter the Great Smoky Mountains National Park from Cherokee. We were only in the vehicles for a few minutes before arriving at the visitor center. Hug-a-Bug was very focused on completing all the tasks to earn her Junior Ranger badge. As soon as she stepped out of the Jeep, she walked past the visitor center entrance and marched ahead of us and around the building. Behind the visitor center was a recreation of a nineteenth-century farm called the Mountain Farm Museum. Hug-a-Bug continued ahead of us all, in search of an answer for her Junior Ranger booklet about early settler's spring houses.

As we walked around the farm, Papa Lewis gave us some of the history.

"According to the National Park Service, the buildings here were moved from other areas in the park to give visitors a feel for early life in the Great Smoky Mountains. The cabin was built out of American chestnut before the chestnut blight," Papa Lewis informed us.

"This is pretty cool that the park brought all these buildings together as an example of early farm life in the Smokies," I said.

Hug-a-Bug rejoined our group, happy that she had found her Junior Ranger answer to the question.

"Before we go, can we stop in the visitor center?" Hug-a-Bug asked as she continued walking, with a bounce in her step, towards the Oconaluftee Visitor Center.

None of us had a chance to ask Hug-a-Bug what the Junior Ranger question and answer was. We all followed her inside. She stepped up to a counter staffed by park rangers and park volunteers. There were several tourists with maps unfolded on the counter, getting expert advice from the park rangers on their Great Smoky Mountain visit. Crockett and I stood nearby while Hug-a-Bug got in line to speak with a park ranger. When Hug-a-Bug reached the front of the line, the park ranger greeted her and asked how he could help. Crockett and I moved our way through the line of people and stood alongside Hug-a-Bug.

"Does anyone work in the park by the name of Will?" Hug-a-Bug asked.

"Hmm. That's funny you ask. There was a volunteer named Will Lewis that worked here up until two months ago. He preferred to be called Wild Bill. He was only on staff for a few months. He interacted great with the park visitors and we hated to see him go. But, he had a fascinating goal he wanted to accomplish. He wanted to explore as many areas of the Smokies as he could, through the eyes of those that lived here before him. The next thing we knew, he left to volunteer as a miller's apprentice."

The three of us looked at each other in disbelief. Hug-a-Bug's idea of checking with the park was a home run. This had to be Papa Lewis' cousin Will. I mean, what are the odds of someone *else* named Will Lewis working here? *This has to be him,* I thought.

"Why do you want to know about Wild Bill?" the park ranger asked.

"We've been trying to locate our papa's long-lost cousin and we think Will Lewis, I mean Wild Bill, might be him," Hug-a-Bug answered.

"What's a miller?" Crockett asked.

"You need to go to the Mingus Mill and see for yourself. Millers worked in the grist mills. Early settlers relied on grist mills to grind corn and wheat. Mingus Mill is just up the road as you go up into the park, on the left-hand side of the road. You can't miss it," the park ranger said.

"Thank you," the three of us said in unison, leaving the counter so that the next person in the growing line could get advice on their own adventure.

"You bet! Good luck! I hope you find Wild Bill."

Our adventure had just changed course. We ran back over to where our parents stood with Papa Lewis and Grandma. When we told Papa that a Will Lewis worked here up until two months ago, a smile spread across his face from ear to ear.

"Will left the visitor center to be a miller's apprentice, and the Mingus Mill is just up the road. He might be there," I explained.

Everyone felt an immediate sense of urgency to find Wild Bill. We all trotted out of the visitor center, got into the vehicles, and drove up the road for about a half mile, heading north of the Oconaluftee Visitor Center. We pulled off of Newfound Gap Road, into a large parking lot. We parked, and hurried along towards the mill.

We approached the Mingus Mill, a three-story structure. A long wooden flume was carrying water from a nearby stream towards the mill. The water was rushing along so hard and so fast it was spilling over the sides. The water flowed along, like a log ride at an amusement park, into the back of the building. Then it poured down onto the notches of a great big turbine wheel, causing it to turn, which then moved the grinding stone that ground the grain in the mill. We stepped inside the mill, unsure if Will would be there. We saw a man wearing denim bib overalls. He was pouring corn from a sack into a wooden hopper. A group of visitors had gathered before him and he introduced himself as the miller.

"That doesn't look like Will," Papa Lewis whispered.

"You haven't seen Will in forty years. Are you sure that's not him?" my dad whispered back.

We all stood and listened to the miller tell the Mingus Mill story. "The Mingus family had Sion Thomas Early build this mill in 1896," the miller stated.

He pointed to a circular stone that was in motion, grinding the corn he had just poured into the wooden hopper, and he said, "The stone was imported from France and was used to grind corn into cornmeal and wheat into flour. This is a unique mill because it has a metal turbine instead of a wooden waterwheel. The finished product spits out into the exit hopper over here," he said, pointing to where a sack had been placed and was filling up with cornmeal.

"People from as far as fifteen miles away brought their corn and wheat to the mill to be ground. They paid the miller by giving him a portion of their grain. The grain was then used to make bread, biscuits, cakes, corn whiskey (a.k.a moonshine), and many other baked goods," the miller said.

The miller continued with his presentation and answered some questions from the other visitors. We waited to approach the miller until he was done talking and the other tourists had walked on to another location.

Papa Lewis asked him, "You don't know a Will Lewis, do you?"

The miller looked up in surprise and said, "You mean Wild Bill? I sure do. Wild Bill worked as my apprentice up until about a month ago, when he left to fill in as the miller at the Cable Mill in Cades Cove. He sure was a great apprentice to work with. I really didn't have to teach him anything—he seemed to already know everything. He was a natural miller. It was as if he had gone back in time and learned from the original Mingus millers."

Papa Lewis smiled.

"Why do you ask?" the miller inquired.

"I think Wild Bill is my long-lost cousin. I last saw him forty years ago," Papa Lewis said.

"What a wonderful man. He had a bucket list that consisted of trying to live the life of various individuals that used to live here in the Smokies."

"That's definitely my cousin. Thank you for all the information," Papa Lewis replied.

"Good luck. I hope you reconnect."

We all walked single-file through the mill and climbed the stairs up to the storage area. We had the room all to ourselves.

"We seem to be one step behind your cousin," I said to Papa Lewis.

"I know. Our best bet is to get over to Cades Cove. If he has a bucket list of people to follow, he may not be a miller for long."

"While we're here, are you thinking what I'm thinking?" I asked, anticipating that everyone would want to see the mill in operation back in the day.

"Let's do it," Crockett said.

We all formed a circle and I placed my hand on the family journal and said, "Take us back to 1897." The mill was built in 1896, but I figured it may have taken a year or so to get up and running. After a few seconds, I felt something heavy push me towards the center of the room. All of us were moved over by piles of heavy sacks of fresh ground flour and cornmeal. The room, empty just seconds before, was now lined with these bags, leaving very little room to stand. We heard lots of chattering voices coming from outside the building. It was a warm summer day, and through the doorway, we saw a few dozen women, men, and children gathered outside in front of the mill. A horse and buggy were sitting out front. We were all wearing different clothing. I had on bib overalls, a cotton shirt, and no shoes. The ladies all wore long dresses. We walked down the steps to where the miller was busy grinding more corn. There was lots of activity going on. Men and boys were carrying bags of unground corn and wheat into the mill as others were leaving with sacks of freshly ground corn and wheat.

Mom whispered to Aunt Walks-a-Lot, "Can you imagine having to ride a horse or walk to the mill, just to get some grain or flour to bake something?"

"Well, at least it was the boys and men that had to carry the grain back and forth. This does make me thankful that I can buy flour and cornmeal at the grocery store."

"It's amazing how the settlers converted water into power. Now, we take electricity for granted," I whispered.

We stepped outside and some people stared at us, never having seen us before, but then they went back to their conversations. I overheard several people bartering. Two men struck a deal. One man swapped a hunting rifle in exchange for two baby pigs. A barefoot teenaged boy traded the chicken he was holding for a hammer. After a few minutes, we wandered back into the mill, back up to the third floor, huddled together, and I took us back to the present. No one spoke until we got out to the parking lot.

"Those people were trading things instead of paying with money," Hug-a-Bug said.

"That's called bartering, Hug-a-Bug. I guess you couldn't just pick up Chipotle or McDonald's in the Smokies back then, huh?" I joked.

"With all the steps they had to go through just to get flour to make a meal, I can safely say that dinner as an early settler was the complete opposite of modern-day fast food," Crockett replied and we all laughed.

"We have quite a drive to get over to Cades Cove. We better head in that direction so we have time to pitch camp and eat dinner," Papa Lewis suggested.

"Are you thinking we can catch up to your cousin Will today?" I asked.

"No, we will have to wait until tomorrow. They close the Cades Cove loop road in the evening. You will get even more of a flavor for early settler life in the Smokies tomorrow, when we explore Cade's Cove."

We all climbed into our respective vehicles and drove north on Newfound Gap Road, up and over the mountain, and down the other side. We turned left off of Newfound Gap Road onto Little River Road and continued for another twenty miles, following the scenic two-lane road, and enjoying views of the Little River. We passed the turnoff to Elkmont and several other sites packed with tourists before arriving at the Cades Cove campground. Another segment of our adventure had ended, and a new one was about to begin.

I had a newfound appreciation for how big the park was. We had started our day in the Cataloochee campground, and now we were ending our day clear across the park in the Cades Cove campground. The Appalachian Trail runs for seventy-one miles along the ridge of the entire length of the park. Even with vehicles to zip around in, it was a long distance to travel on narrow mountain roads. The Smokies is indeed a "great," big national park.

Everyone had a new sense of excitement about catching up with Papa's cousin, Wild Bill. Looking for Wild Bill added an element of the unknown to our trip, which was already the most amazing adventure I'd ever been on, and on top of that, you couldn't ask for a better location to search for someone. From the tranquil mountain streams and beautiful sunsets to the thick forests, wild animals and rich history, this was the perfect backdrop for most anything.

We all worked together setting up camp, and then it was time for dinner. Everyone was hungry. Mom surprised us with a bag of cornmeal she had bought back at the Mingus Mill.

"I thought we could try out some skillet cornbread to go along with our ham, potatoes, and green beans."

We all went about a similar campsite routine to what we had done the night before. We kids gathered firewood and Uncle Boone and Dad got a blazing fire going. Mom, Grandma, and Aunt Walks-a-Lot assembled the meal. Mom used our propane stove to cook. It took longer to prepare the meal than to eat.

You could tell everyone was tired and hungry. Few words were spoken during dinner, and we ate everything—there were no leftovers. After dinner, we sat around the fire for a bit as the sun set and the wooded campground grew dark. Papa Lewis and Grandma were the first to call it a night and slip into the tent. It wasn't more than ten minutes later that the rest of us did the same.

It's funny how nighttime sounds can frighten you, especially if you don't know what's making them. This is especially true when you're camping with nothing more than a thin nylon tent to offer what you know is a false sense of security. As I lay awake in my sleeping bag that night, I heard a chirping bird sound, which Dad had told me the night before was a whippoorwill's call. He said they make their calls at night. So that sound didn't alarm Hug-a-Bug and me as we lay in our sleeping bags. It was the next sound that disrupted my dreamy thoughts drifting into sleep. It was a very distinctive eerie sound:

"Hoo, hoo who, hoo, hoo ahoo!"

"What was that?" Hug-a-Bug asked in a nervous whisper.

"I don't know."

"That's a barred owl," Dad answered. "There are five types of owls in the Smokies: screech, barn, great horned, saw-whet, and barred, and they each have a distinct call."

We could now write off another mystery sound as nothing to worry about. We finally drifted off to sleep.

CHAPTER 12

AWAY FROM IT ALL

Morning came quickly after a much-needed ten hours of sleep. The cool part about camping is that you don't need an alarm clock to wake up—the natural sunlight is Mother Nature's way of opening your eyes to start a new day. The tent walls were beginning to glow with sunlight. As I lay inside our tent, I could hear the muffled voices of other nearby campers, and occasional metal clanks of pots and pans, as people were preparing the first meal of the day.

"Okay, up and at 'em, everyone, we have another big day in store for us," Papa Lewis called out. "We have bike rental reservations to ride the Cades Cove Loop. The road is closed to cars until ten AM. We're going to have a quick breakfast, and we have packed lunches all ready to go."

With that announcement, those of us who were still lazing in our sleeping bags groggily came to life, pulling on pants, tucking in shirts, and lacing up shoes. Everyone quickly took care of their morning routines.

Mom put on some coffee, Aunt Walks-a-Lot handed everyone granola bars, and I helped Dad make sure everyone had water and lunch packed in their daypacks.

As everyone wolfed down breakfast, I unfolded the map of Cades Cove onto the picnic table to get a sense of what we were about to do. Crockett and Hug-a-Bug sat down and joined me. All three of us were scanning the map looking for the grist mill where we hoped we would find Cousin Will. We were looking down at an eleven-mile loop dotted with historic homesteads and churches.

"Here it is," I said, pointing to a spot on the map labeled "Cable Mill Historic Area."

"It looks like that's the only mill in Cades Cove. That has to be it," Crockett said.

"That's over halfway around the loop. It will take us a while to get there on bikes," Hug-a-Bug said.

"Don't worry about Cousin Will. Let's enjoy the day in Cades Cove. There is lots to see and do before we get to the grist mill. If Cousin Will is here, we'll find him," Papa Lewis said.

We picked up our rental bikes and pedaled over to the entrance gate for the Cades Cove Loop road. On Wednesdays and Saturdays, the road is open to non-motorized traffic from seven to ten in the morning, and today was Saturday. We had a three-hour jump on the automobile tourist traffic that usually filled the one-lane road.

A park ranger arrived just before seven, opened the gate, and we were off, pedaling into Cades Cove. We were surrounded by dozens of other cyclists, runners, and walkers taking advantage of the "non-motorized" hours. The bike ride was a nice change after having spent several hours in the car the day before. Shortly after we rode through the gate, the trees lining the road thinned out to reveal expansive meadows and tall mountains off in the distance. Patches of fog lingered above the field, and the sun was peaking over distant mountains with brilliant yellow and red hues adding a colorful light show to the blue morning sky. Scattered deer were grazing the tall thick grass. *Wow, from visiting other areas of the park, I would have never guessed such a flat area of land existed in the Smokies.* Almost everywhere else we had been it was either up or down.

Papa Lewis slowed his bike and stopped along the side of the road overlooking the cove and we all did the same. The road was lined with a simple barbed wire fence with log posts spaced every four or five feet apart.

"Imagine traveling over the mountains looking for a place to settle down and make a farm, and wandering into Cades Cove," Papa Lewis said, as he looked out across the field.

"I'd want to stay," I said.

"Yeah, this place feels like it's your own private playground," Hug-a-Bug added.

"In 1818, the first settlers arrived in the area. They had a vision of what you see today. But what they actually saw back then was flat land covered by forest. They realized the potential to make this into farmland. In 1818, the land still officially belonged to the Cherokee Indians. The Cherokee never settled in Cades Cove; they used it as their hunting ground. Over the years, more and more settlers flowed into Cades Cove to live. They cleared the land by hand to grow crops, carve out roads, and build churches and schools," Papa Lewis explained.

Papa Lewis set off on his bike again, and we all followed, cruising up and down small hills, enjoying the picture-perfect views. We rode past Sparks Lane, one of the original narrow roads that cut across the cove. Soon, we saw a distant cabin off to the right. We all got off our bikes and went over to read the historical sign on the side of the road.

"Hey, Papa Lewis, it says here this is the John Oliver place, and they arrived in 1818. This must be the first settler family you were talking about," I said.

"Yep, that's them."

We all walked a quarter of a mile through a tall grassy field, up to the homestead, which was set back into the tree line. When we got within about thirty yards of the house, we passed through a split rail fence. The fence was made of split tree trunks and branches stacked in a zigzag fashion.

"This was how they constructed fences without having to dig postholes in the rocky ground," Papa Lewis told us.

The cabin was small, not much bigger than my bedroom at home. It had a small loft for sleeping, a front and back porch, and a stone fireplace. Red dirt filled the gaps between the stones of the fireplace, and the cracks between the logs that made up the walls of the cabin.

"Can you imagine living here?" Crockett asked.

"Why imagine?" I replied with a sly grin.

A few other cyclists had just left the cabin and were walking back towards the road. We all walked around the cabin and out of view of the road so no one could see us.

The roadside sign said the house was completed by the early 1820s. So, to play it safe, I took us back to 1825.

My synthetic clothes transformed to cotton pants and shirt, topped with suspenders. A short distance away, there were two tree stumps with boards lying on top. Honey bees were zipping all around the stumps.

"Those are beehives called 'bee gums.' The early settlers didn't have sugar, so they used honey as sweetener instead. They also grew cane and made molasses to use as a sweetener," Papa Lewis explained.

We could hear the clucking noise of chickens coming from a small chicken coop, made out of stacked logs. The grunting of pigs could be heard from the barn off in the distance, next to a corn crib. A bell hanging from the neck of a cow in the field clanged as she stopped chewing grass and looked up at us.

The sweet doughy smell of something baking, mixed in with the scent of wood smoke, caught all of our noses. We all walked around to the front of the cabin, looking for the source. A woman was sitting on the porch stirring something in a tall wooden bucket. She had the bucket wedged between her feet and knees so it wouldn't tip. I spotted the source of the tantalizing smell—a fresh-baked blackberry pie sat cooling on a table up on the porch near the woman. Smoke swirled out of the cabin chimney. A skinned squirrel hung by a string beneath the porch roof. A young girl sat on the porch step staring at us. Next to the little girl sat a toddler-aged boy. He was wearing a dress which at first glance led us to believe he was a she. But I remembered Papa Lewis explaining that all young kids wore dresses back then.

We had obviously caught the woman's attention, but she never stopped her task and continued to churn the wooden stick around in the bucket.

"Y'all must be our new neighbors," the woman said.

"We just arrived in Cades Cove today," I replied, hoping my response was sufficient to explain our presence.

"As soon as I'm done making the butter, I'll serve ya up some fresh corn bread," she said.

"Mighty obliged, ma'am ," I replied, trying to sound like I was actually from 1825, "but we's just passin' through."

"Can we help out with anything?" Hug-a-Bug asked.

"No help needed, thank ya kindly for asking. When we first arrived here in 1818, we nearly starved to death. We could've used some help then. Some Cherokee Indians gave us some food to eat, and that helped, but those first few years was awful lean. By now we got things figured out. My husband John is out in the corn field and should be back in a few hours," the woman told us, then added, "I'm Lucretia Oliver."

"We're the Lewis family," I replied.

"You oughta' stick around for supper. We're fixin' to have a nice meal of squirrel stew, corn, biscuits and blackberry pie."

"Thank ya, ma'am, but we best get goin'."

"Stop back again then."

We raised our hands in farewell and walked around the side of the cabin and out of view. We all huddled together to time-travel back to the present. Once there, we walked back down through the field towards the road, where we had left our bikes.

"The dinner offer sounded good up until she said squirrel stew. Yuck!" Hug-a-Bug said.

"Come on, Hug-a-Bug. It probably tastes like chicken," Dad joked.

"Hug-a-Bug, you'd eat anything that moved back then. The Smokies had plenty of game to eat like squirrel, rabbit, possum, fish, deer, duck, geese, turkey and even bear. They butchered pigs and cattle for meat, too. They would smoke the meat over a fire and cure it with salt to keep it from spoiling. Pork tasted best with that method," Papa Lewis explained.

"I would've liked to taste that fresh butter Mrs. Oliver was making," Uncle Boone said.

"How did they keep butter and milk cold?" Crockett asked.

"Most families would build a little shed over a ground spring. This kind of shed was called a spring house. The cold mountain stream water would run right through the spring house. The family kept things like butter, milk, and eggs in the cold water of the spring—worked as well as any refrigerator," Papa Lewis explained.

"I sure wish we could have had some of that blackberry pie," Crockett said, licking his lips.

"I'd like to know where they got the blackberries from," I said.

"They picked them from the nearby woods. These mountains are loaded with blackberries, huckleberries, elderberries, and raspberries. They also picked other wild food like chestnuts, wild onions, dandelions, and turnip greens," Papa Lewis answered.

"I have to hand it to Lucretia and John Oliver and all the other settlers. I wonder if I could've done it. They worked so hard just to eat and stay alive. Today, we can easily buy all the things that they had to gather and make," Mom said.

"It's unbelievable how far we've come since those days, but I'm sure you would've survived, Petunia (Mom's nickname for her love of flowers). It's in your blood," Aunt Walks-a-Lot said.

We all hopped on our bikes and continued on our journey. We were just a short distance down the road from the John Oliver cabin when Hug-a-Bug called out, "Bears!"

We all turned and looked where Hug-a-Bug was pointing, and off on the right side of the road about thirty yards away were three black bears. It appeared to be a large adult female with her two cubs.

"According to the National Park Service, it's estimated that there are 1,500 black bears in the Great Smoky Mountains National Park. I'm surprised we haven't seen more by now. They're omnivores like us. But they eat more nuts and berries than anything else. For protein, they eat other animals," Papa Lewis informed us.

"Whoa!" Crockett responded.

"We're a little too close. Let's back away slowly and stay close together. You should stay at least fifty yards away, never run or turn away, stick together, and make yourself look as large as possible," Papa Lewis advised.

We all got off our bikes and slowly backed away. The mama bear nudged her cubs up a large oak tree. After we had backed up a safe distance, I pulled out my camera and snapped some great pictures. My zoom lens gave the illusion that we were much closer. Other cyclists stopped next to us and took some pictures, too. We watched the cubs climb down from the tree, then all three bears lumbered into the forest, out of site. We got back on our bikes and continued our tour.

"That was impressive," Aunt Walks-a-Lot said.

"It's much different seeing bears in the wild instead of in cages at the zoo. It's scary, because you don't know what they're going to do," Hug-a-Bug said.

"That's right. They are wild animals and they are unpredictable. If you do what I told you when you see a bear, you should be fine. Never feed them, and if they approach you, raise your hands above you to look bigger, wave your arms, yell, and fight back if it continues to come at you," Papa Lewis added.

"Fight back? How do you fight a black bear?" I asked.

"Stay together. Throw rocks, sticks, hit it with your backpack, jab it with your hiking pole. Spray it with bear spray if you have it. Basically, let it know you won't be an easy meal," Dad replied.

"Black bear attacks on people are extremely rare. Sadly though, careless people feed bears and this leads to their demise. As the saying goes, 'a fed bear is a dead bear.' When a bear learns that if it approaches people it will get food, eventually someone gets hurt and the bear has to be destroyed," Uncle Boone added.

Traveling with such seasoned adventurers like my papa, uncle, and dad was great. Not only had we already learned a ton about the park, but we were also learning bear survival tips.

A short way down the road, we spotted an old church, built from wood and painted white. According to the brochure I picked up at the Cades Cove entrance, this was the Primitive Baptist Church. We all stopped and explored the grounds and building. The wood frame church was built in 1887, replacing the original 1827 log structure. Adjacent to the church, we found a cemetery where some of the original Cades Cove settlers were laid to rest. We wandered the cemetery for a while, examining the old gravestones, before returning to our bikes and continuing our journey.

The Methodist Church came into view on the right side of the road, just a short distance further. Once again, we left our bikes to explore the church and walk through the adjacent cemetery. One thing I had noticed about both cemeteries really disturbed me—there were quite a few children's graves.

"Why are there so many kids' graves in the cemeteries?" I asked Papa Lewis.

"They didn't have all the medical knowledge and skills, or all the medications that we have today. Simple colds and infections that you can easily tackle today could turn deadly back then," Papa Lewis said.

"The Cades Cove tour booklet said that the Primitive Baptist Church closed during the Civil War. That surprised me. I feel so removed from the rest of the world here in Cades Cove—I would think they would've been even more isolated back then. Why would they have had to close the church?" I said.

"You get the illusion that you're cut off from the world here because you're surrounded by the mountains. But there were several roads leading in and out of Cades Cove, and the residents remained connected with the outside world. The Civil War divided our country into two sides. The war split families, friends, churches and entire communities, and sadly, many people died. There are even Civil War soldiers buried in some of the Cades Cove church cemeteries," Papa Lewis replied.

We continued our ride and stopped next at the Elijah Oliver cabin. A plaque out front told us he was the son of John and Lucretia Oliver. We had just met his mom, Lucretia, when we time-traveled. Elijah must have been the toddler on the porch. His cabin was very similar in construction to that of his parents, but with a few upgrades. He had a guest house built into the front porch, which Papa told us was called a "stranger room," and not far from the main house we found the spring house where he would have kept his milk, eggs, and butter cold using the mountain stream water. Very ingenious.

We rode on, approaching a turnoff leading to the Abrams Falls trailhead. Earlier, we had talked about hiking this trail at some point during our visit. We all pulled over to the side of the road to decide whether or not to hike it now. As we looked at the map, we realized that we were just a short distance from the Cable Mill where we hoped to find Cousin Will. The suspense of finding out if Papa Lewis' cousin was at the Cable Mill swayed the group in favor of putting off the Abrams Falls Trail for another day. It was unanimous; everyone agreed to head straight for the Cable Mill. We rode on, picking up the pace, eager to find Cousin Will.

CHAPTER 13

THE SMOKY MOUNTAIN BIATHLON!

We turned off the loop road and into a parking area for the Cades Cove Visitor Center. The parking lot was empty except for some other cyclists that had stopped to tour the grounds and use the restrooms. There were several buildings spread out around the sprawling grounds. Some of the buildings were not original to the site—they had been relocated from other parts of Cades Cove. The visitor center and the blacksmith shop were added later to enhance the tourist experience. But the Cable Mill is the original grist mill, in the same exact same spot where it was built by John P. Cable in 1870. Back then, there were several grist mills that operated in Cades Cove, but this is the only one remaining. We parked our bikes and walked along, following a sign directing us to the Cable Mill. Up ahead, we easily picked out the mill, a two-story wood frame building with a flume carrying water from a mountain stream, similar to the Mingus Mill, with the exception of the large water wheel on the side of the building. The water was spilling down into the waterwheel buckets and the weight of the water was turning the waterwheel.

We walked single-file into the Cable Mill and found the miller hard at work grinding corn. We were the only visitors in the mill, and we approached the miller, hoping it would be Cousin Will.

"Hi y'all, welcome to the Cable Mill," the miller greeted us.

"Are you Wild Bill?" I asked, getting right to the point.

"No, Wild Bill filled in for me until today. He did a great job, too, almost as if he was a miller in his previous life. Why do you ask?"

"He's my Papa Lewis' cousin, and we've been trying to find him ever since we heard that he was in the park. We've been to the Oconaluftee Visitor Center, the Mingus Mill, and now here."

"I reckon he's far up in the mountains by now. Wild Bill said now that his miller skills were no longer needed he was going to walk in the footsteps of Horace Kephart. He had a list of historical figures from the Smokies and he planned, as he put it, to 'walk in their shoes.' "

"Did Wild Bill leave you his cell number?" Crockett asked the miller.

"He doesn't have a phone. If you met him, you would think you were talking to someone from the 1940s. He dresses in clothing from that era, similar to what that guy is wearing," The miller said, pointing at Papa Lewis.

"You say Will, I mean, Wild Bill, was heading up in the mountains today?" Papa Lewis asked the miller.

"That's what he said. He was going to explore where Horace Kephart once stayed in the park."

"Thank you kindly," Papa Lewis said.

"Thanks for the information," I said.

"Here's our contact information. If you see Wild Bill, can you give him this and tell him his cousin is trying to locate him?" Dad asked, handing the miller a piece of paper.

"I sure will. Good luck."

We walked outside and followed the flume back to an old barn to discuss the situation out of earshot of other cyclists.

"I think I know exactly where Wild Bill is going. We can catch up to him, but we have to move fast," Papa Lewis said.

"We've been one step behind Wild Bill ever since we found out he's here. What makes you think we can catch him now?" I asked.

"Until now, we've been days and even weeks behind Wild Bill. Now, we are only a half day behind him."

I pulled the park map out of my daypack, and unfolded it. Crockett grabbed one end and held it while I held the other end.

"Where are you talking about, Papa?" I asked.

Papa stepped over to the map held up between Crockett and me, and everyone gathered around.

"Horace Kephart lived for a short time in a cabin near the Hazel Creek Trail. Right in here," Papa Lewis said, pointing to the area of the map where the Hazel Creek Trail and the Jenkins Ridge Trail meet, over the mountain on the North Carolina side. He traced his finger along the Appalachian Trail and pointed at Derrick Knob Shelter. "Kephart spent the summer of 1906 at Hall Cabin near this shelter. It was used by cattle herders, but it's no longer there. If Wild Bill's retracing Kephart's steps, he will definitely be at one of these two spots."

"That's a lot of ground to cover. Do you plan on hiking in?" Hug-a-Bug asked.

"Well, Hug-a-Bug, this is your opportunity to hike on the Appalachian Trail. We should split into two groups. One group will hike up the Anthony Creek Trail from Cades Cove to the Spence Field Shelter, then head north on the AT to Derrick Knob shelter. I'll go with that group. The other group will ride horses up the Anthony Creek Trail and down the other side of the mountain on the Jenkins Creek Trail to the Havel Creek area. This way we can hit both areas in the park where Kephart lived, and we'll be on the same trails Wild Bill is most likely hiking," Papa Lewis explained

"Where are we going to find horses?" Grandma asked.

Grandma was probably worried about all that hiking. She has a bad knee and was probably planning to join the group going by horseback.

"I have an old friend in Townsend, near Cades Cove, that owns horses. He rides them in the park. We can look him up. We should get moving. We have to get our hiking provisions ready before we go, and we need to get backcountry reservations for the shelters and campsites," Papa said.

Our Cades Cove adventure had just taken an unexpected twist. We walked back to the bikes and rode the remainder of the loop. The weather was great: not too hot and not too cool, with plenty of sunshine. The gates were now open to cars, but the cars had not caught up to us yet, so we still had an open road. We passed by more historic barns, cabins, and picturesque, fence-lined grassy fields. We rounded a bend in the road and encountered three wild turkeys. They were scratching the ground for food and were not bothered by our presence, making it obvious they weren't afraid of hunters. Turkeys are some of the largest birds in the country, and they were an impressive sight to see up close. I took a few pictures, and then we continued riding towards the campground.

I rode up alongside Papa Lewis and asked, "What's the story on Horace Kephart?"

"Horace Kephart was a well-known travel writer who helped establish the Great Smoky Mountains National Park. He wrote some popular books, *Our Southern Highlanders,* and *Camping and Wood Craft: A Guidebook For Those Who Travel in the Wilderness.* That second one, as you can well imagine, really came in handy for folks back then. *Our Southern Highlanders* was about the people who lived in the Great Smoky Mountains. Kephart was a successful librarian. But he had a deep passion to explore the last of the eastern wilderness. So he up and left his family, and moved to the Smokies. He lived among the locals up in the Smokies before it became a park. When he saw the devastation from the logging, he used his writing fame to persuade others to support the creation of the park. He partnered with a photographer, George Masa, and together they created compelling brochures that were used to persuade others to support the creation of the park. He also helped map the Appalachian Trail through the Great Smoky Mountains."

"Wow! He sounds like he was quite an adventurer."

"He was. Unfortunately, he was killed in a car accident before the Smokies officially became a national park."

We arrived back at our campsite by midday. We all ate lunch and discussed plans.

"We need a head count of who is going to hike and who is going to go on horseback," Papa Lewis said.

Uncle Boone and Aunt Walks-a-Lot walked over to the open tailgate of their Land Rover and conversed with each other as they fumbled through some of the gear piled in the back of the car. The rest of us remained seated at the picnic table.

"I want to hike," Crockett said.

"Me too," Hug-a-Bug said.

"Same here," I said.

"I'll ride," Grandma said.

Uncle Boone and Aunt Walks-a-Lot walked back over to the picnic table where we were gathered. Uncle Boone handed Crockett a bright blue backpack stuffed full of provisions with trekking poles strapped to the side and a hydration hose dangling from the top of the pack.

"We're going to ride with Grandma. It'll be fun. I'll get my hiking fix on Mt. Le Conte later, before we leave the park," Aunt Walks-a-Lot said.

"I'll ride along with Grandma and you guys. This will be a good opportunity for Lewis and Clark to backpack together," Mom said.

"Okay, I'll make shelter reservations for the five of us," Dad said.

Papa Lewis gave Uncle Boone the contact information for his horse owner friends in Townsend and reviewed maps and plans with him. Uncle Boone said goodbye to us, hopped in his Range Rover, backed out of the camp-site, and off he went. Dad walked up to the campground office to make shelter reservations while Papa Lewis, Hug-a-Bug, and I replenished our backpacks with food and snacks for three days, and filled up our water contain-ers. Crockett's pack was all set so he sat idle, waiting for us to go.

When Dad returned with our shelter permits, Papa Lewis reviewed plans with everyone.

"We're going to hike up to the Spence Field shelter and stay the night. The horseback riding team will stay here at the campground tonight and head up the mountain in the morning. With horses, they'll be traveling faster than us. They'll ride down the other side of the mountain to the old copper mine in the Hazel Creek area where Kephart once lived. While they're looking for Wild Bill at the copper mine, we'll hike towards the Derrick Knob shelter, where an old rancher's hut that Kephart once stayed at used to be."

Papa pulled out two satellite phones from a haversack and handed one to Grandma. He put the other one in his vintage canvas backpack. Based on his 1940s era clothing, you would get the impression that Papa Lewis would not be up to date with technology, so the high-tech satellite phones surprised us. The satellite phones were smart for what we were about to do. Cellular phones are unreliable in the mountains, but a satellite phone can make contact from anywhere as long as you have open sky. This would allow our two teams to communicate. Our search plan to find Wild Bill was as organized as any professional search team could be.

"We'll wait until tomorrow morning to turn on our satellite phones, to preserve the battery power. When each team reaches their destination, or finds Wild Bill— whichever comes first—they are to call the other team and report in," Papa Lewis explained.

Crockett, Hug-a-Bug, and I hugged our moms and Grandma goodbye, slipped on our backpacks, cinched down the straps, clipped our hip belts together, grabbed our hiking poles, waved a final goodbye, and marched out of the campground with "Lewis" and "Clark" toward the Anthony Creek Trail.

CHAPTER 14

OVER THE HILLS AND THROUGH THE WOODS

It was a little less than five miles to the Spence Field Shelter. We found the Anthony Creek Trail at the back of the picnic area adjacent to the campground. The trail followed a creek, which added the soothing sound of flowing water. We passed through the Anthony Creek horse camp where Uncle Boone, Aunt Walks-a-Lot, Grandma, and Mom would begin their ride in the morning. The trail was framed by newly bloomed pink and white rhododendrons.

"The white rhododendrons are called Rosebay and the pink flowers are referred to as Catawba," Papa Lewis told us.

The hike went smoothly and we soon reached a trail junction. We stopped and drank some water, and I pulled out my map to confirm which way to go. We took a left toward the Bote Mountain Trail and the incline began to get steeper. Papa Lewis and Dad were hiking behind me and Crockett and Hug-a-Bug were ahead of me. Crockett had to put more effort into each step due to his bad leg. His leg brace was a visible reminder of his added struggle to walk, but it didn't slow him down or seem to bother him. He was leading us at a good pace, and he was in good shape. Even if he had walked slower, I wouldn't have minded. As a matter of fact, I was going at my full pace just to keep up! You could tell he was raised by a mom named Walks-a-Lot and a dad named Boone! We walked past a campsite and turned right onto the Bote Mountain Trail in our final approach up to the fabled Appalachian Trail, and then to our shelter for the night. We passed through a tunnel of rhododendron, as if it were a rite of passage before summiting onto the AT.

I had to wipe the sweat dripping from my forehead to keep it out of my eyes as I continued to put one foot in front of the other. We hiked for a while longer and at last the terrain began to level off. We had reached the Appalachian Trail. The wind whistled in my ears as gusts blew over the top of the mountain. It was noticeably cooler up on the mountain than it had been at the campground. Thick, low-hanging clouds moved through the trees. We kept walking and soon came to another trail intersection. A post with two wooden signs jutted out of the ground. We paused to confirm our directional bearings. One sign read "Appalachian Trail" and the other sign read "Eagle Creek Trail." The Spence Field shelter was just 0.2 miles down the Eagle Creek Trail, so we all continued in that direction. Tall, thick grass edged the well-worn dirt trail. Interspersed among the trees in every direction was mountain laurel in full bloom showing off its pink and white flowers.

"This is one of the perks of hiking this time of year. You get to see the mountain laurel and the rhododendrons bloom," Papa Lewis said.

"Papa, why is grass growing up here? It's like a field on top of the mountain," Hug-a-Bug asked.

"James Spence cleared this area to graze sheep and cattle. He had a cabin up here. The forest has reclaimed most of it, but the Park Service maintains some of the grassy parts. The Spence Field shelter, where we're headed, is named after the Spence family," Papa Lewis explained.

Crockett and Hug-a-Bug stopped and turned back to me. Without saying a word, I knew exactly what they were thinking: was I planning to time-travel?

"Guys, I'm tired and hungry. I just want to get to the shelter, take this pack off, and eat. Can we save the time-travel for later?" I asked.

"Sounds good, Bubba Jones," Crockett responded.

"Yeah, I'm bushed too," Hug-a-Bug replied.

"Since this morning, we've biked eleven miles and backpacked almost five. I would say that qualifies as a biathlon," I said.

"Yep, we've all had a big day. I think some food and a good night's rest will do us some good," Dad said.

"You guys are doing great! I've never traveled with better adventurers," Papa Lewis chimed in from the back of our single-file line along the trail.

"I think we're here," Crockett shouted.

Up ahead we could see a small structure with walls of stone. A feeling of relief washed over me, knowing we had reached our camp for the night. My feet felt like they were on fire and my entire body was spent. We walked towards the shelter, eager to take our packs off and settle in. The closer we got to the shelter, the more inviting it looked. It had three stone walls and a fireplace with a stone chimney on one end, which we could see from outside because one wall was completely missing. The entire front of the shelter was open to the great outdoors—no doors or windows needed. A roofed porch provided a place to gather for protection from rain and snow. Posts supported the roof shelter, and there were skylights that allowed natural daylight to illuminate the inside of the shelter. Wooden benches surrounded the posts in front. Inside the three stone walls were two rows of wooden bunks, which could in total sleep ten people comfortably. A fire ring was located in front of the shelter, and as at all shelters and backcountry campsites in the Smokies, there was a cable pulley system in place to hang our food bags and toiletries high in the air, safely out of reach of bear paws.

We all dropped our packs and sat down. Papa Lewis and Dad went to work laying out their sleeping pads and sleeping bags.

"Hey Clark, what bunk do you want?" Papa Lewis asked Dad.

"It doesn't matter."

"I'll take the end bunk here, Clark, why don't you take the other end?"

"Sounds like a plan, Dad."

Hug-a-Bug, Crockett, and I rolled out our sleeping pads and sleeping bags on the upper bunks. Then we all changed out of our sweaty hiking clothes and into dry outfits. Crockett and Hug-a-Bug volunteered to go pump water out of the nearby spring. I came along to fill a pan with water to use for dinner. The water was coming out of the rocks through a pipe and formed a small puddle between some rocks, then trickled down the mountain in a small stream. This was probably the water source the Spence family had used when they lived up here. We walked back to the shelter, where Dad had already set up our one-burner hiking stove. I put the pot of water on the burner, and Dad gave his gas canister a few pumps, turned the fuel knob on, and lit the stove with a lighter. A blue flame flared up. Dad adjusted the fuel lever and in five minutes the little flame brought our pot of water to a boil. We had three packages of freeze-dried lasagna dinners already open and lined up. I poured an equal amount of water into each package, then resealed the tops. Ten minutes later, we all sat down on the log benches eating lasagna and sipping some lemonade that Hug-a-Bug had made.

We cleaned up our dishes, brushed our teeth, went to the bathroom, and we were all zipped into our sleeping bags by dark.

"Is this where the thru-hikers stay on the Appalachian Trail?" Hug-a-Bug asked.

"Yep. There are three-walled shelters similar to this one, spaced every ten miles or so for the entire length of the Appalachian Trail," Dad answered.

That was the only conversation we had before all fading off to sleep, with a nice cool mountain breeze wafting in over us—until a noise outside the shelter woke me up. I looked at my watch; it was four-thirty in the morning.

In the dimly moonlit shelter I could see the silhouettes of Crockett and Hug-a-Bug sitting up in their sleeping bags, awoken by the noise as well. There it went again. Somewhere out in front of the shelter, we could hear something tearing the grass up from the ground.

"What is that?" Crockett whispered.

"I don't know," I whispered. I imagined some man-eating beast circling our shelter, waiting for the perfect moment to pounce.

I grabbed my headlamp, turned it on and aimed it out into the darkness, illuminating the source of the noise: five deer standing just a few feet from the shelter. They froze in the light for a minute and then returned to eating grass. With each bite, they pulled the grass up, tearing it out of the ground.

"It's just deer," I whispered, with a chuckle.

We all lay back down to sleep. I must have dozed off into a deep sleep once again, because the next thing I knew, it was daylight, and Papa Lewis and Dad were boiling water for coffee, and preparing freeze-dried eggs for breakfast. We were literally in a fog. The air was filled with a cool mist which limited our visibility to just a few feet. I felt refreshed as I unzipped from my sleeping bag. Crockett and Hug-a-Bug were both sitting up in their sleeping bags staring out into the fog.

"I slept great," Hug-a-Bug declared. She jumped down from the top bunk.

"I always sleep better in the cool mountain air," Papa Lewis chimed in. He was sitting with Dad, sipping on his morning coffee.

We joined Lewis and Clark for some eggs, hot cocoa, and granola bars. Then we all changed into our hiking clothes, deflated our sleeping pads, stuffed our sleeping bags and gear into our backpacks, used the privy, and were on the trail by eight AM. Papa Lewis turned on his satellite phone and clipped it to the shoulder strap of his backpack.

Hug-a-Bug led the way along the Eagle Creek Trail back towards the Appalachian Trail. We reached the trail junction and turned right, heading north on the AT towards the Derrick Knob Shelter, in pursuit of Wild Bill. We had a little over six miles to go. We would hike over the famous "Rocky Top" and Thunderhead Mountains along the way.

Hug-a-Bug stopped suddenly on the trail. A few feet ahead of her stood a stout, dark-haired, short-legged animal. It resembled a pig, but looked more like the big, bad wolf than one of the three little pigs. Its snout was much longer than Old McDonald's pig. On either side of its snout were sharp tusks that could easily stab any one of us. Its tail was straight instead of curly. The ground beneath Hug-a-Bug's feet looked like it had been freshly plowed. This beast had completely torn up the trail and surrounding area. It stared at us for a few seconds, and then trotted off into the forest.

"What was that?" Hug-a-Bug asked tremulously.

"That was a wild boar. European boar were brought to the U.S. to stock game reserves. But a bunch of them escaped into the Great Smoky Mountains, and have adapted and multiplied. They're not native to the park and, as you can see, they tear up the land. They also carry disease, and they destroy the habitat and food sources for the native species. The Park Rangers actively remove the wild boars through trapping and hunting," Papa Lewis explained.

We continued down the trail. The fog began to lift and we once again enjoyed some blue sky in the Smokies. The trees thinned out and gave way to grassy balds and spectacular views. We climbed up to Rocky Top and took a few pictures of the stunning view—nothing but green, forested mountains for miles.

"Hey guys, did Papa Lewis tell you that your left foot is in Tennessee and your right foot is in North Carolina?" Dad asked.

"It's true. Here in the Great Smoky Mountains National Park, the Appalachian Trail is the state line between Tennessee and North Carolina," Papa Lewis added.

"Cool!" I said imagining a dotted line on the trail between my left foot and my right.

We continued on up to Thunderhead and climbed up a mound of stones and enjoyed the most amazing view in every direction. After we spent time on top of Thunderhead, we continued down the AT.

We finally reached the Derrick Knob Shelter around eleven AM, our eyes eagerly scanning the area for Wild Bill. To our great disappointment, the shelter was empty, with no sign that anyone had been there recently. We were beginning to think we might never catch up with Wild Bill. We took off our packs and sat down for a break. Everyone took out a snack and sipped on their water. I gnawed on a chocolate chip energy bar. Papa Lewis walked back onto the trail to get a clear view up to the sky for a satellite signal, and called Grandma. I could hear him explain that we had reached our destination, but had not found Wild Bill. You could tell Grandma was explaining what they had found from the other end as he nodded his head and listened. After a few minutes, he took the phone away from his ear, folded up the antenna and walked back over to where we sat. We eagerly waited for Papa to tell us what the other team had found.

"Boone, Walks-a-Lot, Petunia, and Grandma rode up and over the mountain at dawn this morning, led by a guide. About an hour ago, they reached the area where Kephart once lived, but no one was there. They said half-burnt logs were in the fire ring, and someone may have camped there as recently as two nights ago. Now, they're heading back over the mountain to Cades Cove," Papa Lewis explained.

"So now what?" I asked in frustration.

"Yeah, we've chased Wild Bill clear across this park and we still haven't found him," Hug-a-Bug added.

"I'm as frustrated as anyone. I just can't ... " Papa Lewis stopped talking mid-sentence.

Something was moving towards us from the northeast. We could hear bushes shake and rocks click as they were being stepped on. It was not on the trail though, which led us to believe the source of the noise might be a large animal rather than a person.

"Shhhhh," Papa Lewis whispered as everyone silently clustered together facing the direction of the sound.

The sound drew closer to us as we stood in front of the Derrick Knob Shelter.

Dad stepped in front of us and shouted, "Who goes there? Hello."

CHAPTER 15

You Can Hike But You Cannot Hide!

S uddenly, a man emerged from the thick entangle-ment of bushes and rhododendron, and stepped onto the trail, a short distance from where we all stood. He was dressed like an outdoorsman from the 1940s, wearing a button-down, long-sleeve Oxford shirt, and a pair of khaki military pants similar to Papa Lewis'. He had a World War II-era leather ammo pouch on his hip belt.

"Well, hello! I was nosing around the area and heard you call out," the man said.

"Will? Wild Bill?" Papa Lewis asked, stepping towards the man.

"What? Fred? Is that you?! What are you doing out here?!" (Papa Lewis' first name is Fred, although it is only seen on paper and pretty much never spoken.)

Papa Lewis walked up to the man, and they embraced each other in a bear hug and smacked each other on the back.

"It's been forty years, Will. Look at you," Papa Lewis said.

"I know. Where has all the time gone?" Wild Bill asked.

"This is my family," Papa said to Wild Bill.

Papa pointed to each of us as he introduced us. "This is my son, Clark; my grandson, Bubba Jones; my grandson, Crockett; and my granddaughter, Hug-a-Bug."

"Nice to meet all of you. I'll bet you've had some great adventures with your grandfather," Wild Bill said.

"Our current adventure has been finding you," I said to Wild Bill.

"I'm impressed that you did. Right now, I'm retracing the steps of Horace Kephart," Wild Bill said.

"We know. We've been tracking you since you left the Oconaluftee Visitor Center," Hug-a-Bug said.

"Well, last night I stayed at Silers Bald, and the night before that, I camped down on the Little Fork, near an old copper mine where Kephart once lived. This shelter here is very close to the Hall Cabin, a herder's cabin where, according to the records, Kephart spent the summer of 1907. I was looking off-trail for the original foundation when I heard you guys."

"We've been retracing Kephart's steps to find you. We split into two groups. The other half of our family rode down to the Little Fork area on horseback this morning, looking for you. I just spoke with them by satellite phone. We hiked to the Derrick Knob shelter, predicting that you would be at one of those locations," Papa Lewis explained.

"A satellite phone? Wow, Fred, you've come a long way," Wild Bill said.

"They work in the backcountry, and it helped us find you," Papa Lewis responded, a bit defensively.

"Do you all want to camp here with me tonight at Derrick Knob Shelter?" Wild Bill asked.

"That would be great. We already have shelter reservations."

We unfolded the park map and decided that tomorrow morning we would retrace our steps south on the AT, back to Cades Cove. Wild Bill agreed to hike back with us in the morning. Papa Lewis called Grandma on the satellite phone and shared the news about finding Wild Bill, and explained that we would see them tomorrow afternoon back at camp.

It was fascinating to meet Papa's time-travel counterpart and to listen to the two of them interact. It was as if they had picked up their conversation where it left off the last time they saw each other forty years ago.

"They know all about our family time travel, Will. As a matter of fact, Bubba Jones has taken over my skill. I passed it off to him at campsite #24, the same place where you and I went with Grandpa," Papa Lewis was saying to Will.

"Boy, it's as if that happened yesterday. It is time to hand over the skills to the next in line, isn't it? It's been forty years. I don't have any kids or grandkids, is the problem, though. I never married."

After a short while of small talk and some lunch, we had all reenergized and were ready for some exploration.

"Let me show you where I think the Hall Cabin was," Wild Bill suggested.

We secured our food and toiletries up onto the bear-proof cables, and then followed Wild Bill into the woods. Wild Bill stopped a short way in, and pointed out the foundation remnants of the Hall Cabin.

"Do you want to travel back and meet Kephart?" Wild Bill asked.

"That would be great!" I said.

"Let me do the honors, Bubba Jones," Wild Bill said as he opened up the leather ammo pouch on his hip belt and removed a small waterproof map case.

"We need to be very careful when we go back. Kephart documented everything. We don't want to stand out to him, or we could alter history," Wild Bill cautioned.

We circled around Wild Bill.

He clutched his map case in his hand and said, "Take us back to the summer of 1907."

Seconds later, the trees were gone, replaced by a meadow on top of the mountain. A log cabin with a wood-shingled roof appeared on the nearby foundation. It had two stone chimneys, one at either end. The door was front and center with a window to the right of the door. The sky was overcast and we were being pelted with a cold hard rain.

"Kephart is here for the summer," Wild Bill whispered.

No sooner had Wild Bill spoken when a man emerged from the cabin. He wore a wide-brimmed fedora, a long-sleeve shirt, long pants, and a handkerchief tied around his neck. He had a pistol in a leather shoulder holster strapped to his side, and he was smoking a tobacco pipe.

It was rainy and cold, so Kephart stuck close to the front door of the cabin.

Wild Bill led us out of sight from Kephart and into the tree line.

"I'm afraid to risk altering history by interacting with Kephart. He wrote about literally every single person he met up here. We'd better get back to the present," Wild Bill said, placing his hand on his map case.

In seconds we were once again surrounded by woods, the cabin was gone, and I could see the modern Derrick Knob shelter. We all walked back to it.

Wild Bill asked Papa Lewis if they could have a private conversation. They two of them walked away from the shelter and out of our earshot. After a few minutes, we saw Papa Lewis pull out his satellite phone, dial a number, and converse with someone. Then they turned and came back to the shelter.

"Crockett, I would be honored to pass my time-travel ability on to you. Your Papa Lewis checked with your parents just now on the satellite phone, and we all agree that you would be a great choice. Would you like to receive this privilege?" Wild Bill asked.

Crockett's eyes opened wide, and a big smile spread across his face. "Boy, would I! It would be an honor."

Wild Bill removed the leather ammo pouch from his belt and handed it over to Crockett.

"I hereby bestow my time-travel skills to you. Since you already know that this skill is to be used only for outdoor exploration in our parks and wild lands, I won't bore you with all the details," Wild Bill said to Crockett.

"Thank you!" Crockett said as he clenched the ammo pouch with both hands, gazing down at it.

Crockett unbuckled the flap on the ammo pouch and pulled out the map. Crockett examined the ammo pouch a moment before pulling out the map case and unfolding it. His facial expression turned from a smile to a wide-eyed look of surprise.

"Hey, Bubba Jones, Hug-a-Bug, look what's in here!"

Inside the waterproof cover was the missing half of the cipher code.

"Wild Bill, did you ever wonder where the other half of this coded message was?" I asked, pointing at the weathered half piece of paper in the map case.

In my excitement, I didn't even give Wild Bill time to respond as I continued, "We have the other half of this coded message!"

Crockett carefully removed the torn piece of paper from the map case and unfolded it. I did the same with the half-sheet from our family journal. We laid them together on a shelter bunk. The pieces were a perfect match. I pulled out my camera and snapped a picture of the complete message.

"When your Papa Lewis and I inherited our time-travel skills from our grandfather forty years ago, he gave me this map along with this torn piece of paper. I figured he must have given your Papa Lewis the other half. I think he wanted us to work together to decipher this message," Wild Bill explained.

"What could be so secret that it was written in code?" I asked.

"Imagine if our time-travel skills got into the hands of someone with bad intentions. You could really mess up history with these skills. I believe Grandpa separated this message as a precaution, and he figured that one day we would bring the pieces together and decipher it," Papa Lewis said.

"Now that we have the full message, we need to decipher it," I said.

"We need a key or a cipher wheel to decode it, Bubba Jones," Crockett said.

"That's our next hurdle—cracking the code," I said. Dinner time came fast, and we all worked together to prepare a freeze-dried meal. As the sun set behind the mountains, we all sat up and listened to Papa Lewis and Wild Bill share their adventures. But even with all the excitement of wild adventures, time-traveling, and unsolved ciphers, everyone was bone-tired, and we soon crawled into our sleeping bags and drifted off to sleep.

Everyone was up at the crack of dawn. I knew, from the sound of Dad's one-burner stove hissing, that Dad was up and preparing his morning coffee. After a granola bar breakfast, we packed up and hit the trail, backtracking towards Cades Cove with Wild Bill in tow. The hike along the AT went surprisingly fast, and we reached the Bote Mountain Trail junction to Cades Cove in a couple of hours.

Wild Bill was fun to hike with. He knew loads of facts and trivia, just like Papa Lewis. He'd spent much of his life in the Great Smoky Mountains, though he'd had plenty of other adventures. He had hiked all the trails in the park, which made him known in those parts as a "900-miler."

On the descent down the mountain, Crockett was leading the pack, and I was lost in thought behind him, when all of the sudden Wild Bill hollered out,

"Crockett! Stop! Don't take another step." Wild Bill ran up to Crockett, who had followed instructions and was frozen in place. Wild Bill pointed down at the ground a few feet in front of him and said, "We are the luckiest hikers on the trail today. The Great Smoky Mountains have twenty-three types of snakes, according to the National Park service. Only two are poisonous. The one coiled up right there next to the trail is one of the poisonous ones, a timber rattlesnake. They are aggressive, and they will bite."

We stepped back slowly from the snake and waited to see if it would leave the side of trail.

"The only other poisonous snake in this area is the copperhead. Those are usually found at lower elevations near streams," Wild Bill explained.

"I'm genuinely interested in most reptiles. I like turtles and lizards. But for some reason, I don't feel so lucky about meeting one of the two poisonous snakes here in the park," Hug-a-Bug said.

"Can I just say that I hate snakes?" I said.

"Don't knock them. They play an important part in the ecosystem and it's rare to see them," Wild Bill replied.

The timber rattler slithered off into the brush, and we continued our descent to Cades Cove. We turned off of the Bote Mountain Trail and started down the Anthony Creek Trail, and soon the trail began to follow Anthony Creek.

"Did you know that this park is considered the salamander capital of the world? It's true; look it up. There are over thirty species in the park," Wild Bill explained with excitement. "Let me show you. Follow me and watch your step." He led us off the trail to the stream.

Wild Bill showed us how to look under rocks near the stream by pulling the rock up so the gap faced away, giving snakes or other creatures a safe escape. He taught us to use a plastic bag or container to pick up the salamanders. Touching a salamander with our bare hands can dry out their skin, and he instructed us to gently return the overturned rock to its original position. I pulled up a rock, and a red flash darted out from underneath it.

"That's a black-chinned red salamander," Wild Bill said.

We didn't find any other creatures, and got back on the trail after exploring a short while. We made good time, reaching the campground by lunchtime. Papa Lewis introduced Wild Bill to Boone, Aunt Walks-a-Lot, Petunia, and Grandma.

As we ate lunch, Wild Bill explained how following in the footsteps of some of the early Great Smoky Mountains residents and park creators helped him appreciate the land and the people even more. He shared his latest adventure: the pursuit of Horace Kephart. He explained that Kephart served as a spokesperson for preserving and protecting the park. What he admired most about Kephart was how he went from city slicker to outdoorsman. He took up life in the Smokies, living among the mountain folk, and recorded how they lived, how they talked, and pretty much everything else about their culture. He explained that Kephart's writings preserved a culture that no longer exists in the park, because when the Great Smoky

Mountain National Park was created, the thousands of residents that called the Smokies home had to leave.

"It makes me sad to think that all those people lost their homes to make this a park," Hug-a-Bug said.

"Everyone was paid for their land. There were two deals offered to the residents. You were offered 100% market value for your property or fifty percent of the value and a lifetime lease to continue living on your land. Some of the residents were happy to sell and move, and were given market value for their property, while others were deeply saddened to leave their homes. It was a difficult time for many, but it was an exciting time for many others. Lots had to be done to make this into a national park. Let's take a ride into Cades Cove. I want to show you something," Wild Bill said.

We all hopped into the vehicles and drove out of the campground and onto the loop road. Most of us were too exhausted from the hike to even think about walking anymore today, but that wasn't what Wild Bill had in mind. Dad drove for a few miles until Wild Bill instructed us to pull off the road near the Missionary Baptist Church. We stepped out of our vehicles and Wild Bill led us over to a large circle of stones.

"This is all that remains of a Civilian Conservation Corps—or CCC, as it came to be known—camp that was once here in Cades cove. This was one of several CCC camps throughout the park. The CCC was known as 'Roosevelt's Tree Army.' The CCC built this park. It was one of their biggest operations. In 1932, the country was in a deep depression. Many people had lost their jobs. President Roosevelt created the CCC to put people back to work. Crockett, it's time to try out your time-travel skills. Take us back to 1933, at 0600."

Crocket clutched the map case and said, "Let's go to 1933, at exactly 0600."

A second later, our ears were blasted by the reveille blaring from a nearby trumpet. Men dressed in military uniforms were barking out orders. Lights flickered on inside wooden barracks and hundreds of men wearing the same khaki uniforms emerged and lined up in formation.

"Where are we?" Crockett whispered.

"We are in a CCC camp. The CCC had to follow military rules in camp, but they would leave camp each day to go to various work sites throughout the park. The Park Service supervised the CCC at the worksites. They built roads, trails, bridges, the shelters along the AT, and they restored the historic buildings here in Cades Cove," Wild Bill explained. "Hey, Crockett, take us back to the present before we're discovered. They're about to do morning calisthenics and I'm too tired for that today."

"Take us back to the present," Crocket said, holding the map case.

The barracks, the formation of CCC enrollees, and the camp commanders barking out orders were gone; just the stone circle remained against the tranquil backdrop of Cades Cove.

"The CCC brought together young men from all walks of life together to build this park. The jobs they did in the park gave them career skills. They learned to farm, plant trees, build roads and bridges, construct buildings, and build fish hatcheries. Some of them even learned to read and write," Wild Bill explained.

Near where we stood was a stone maker with a bronze plaque attached to it that read, "In Honor of the Civilian Conservation Corps 1933–1942, whose hands built the roads, trails, bridges, campgrounds, and picnic areas in Great Smoky Mountains National Park for the benefit and enjoyment of the people. If you seek their monument, look about you. Dedicated September 27, 2008."

We drove back to camp and rested up for our next park adventure.

CHAPTER 16

TOTALLY WORTH THE TRIP!

We stayed in the park for another week. Wild Bill fit right in with our family, and between him and Papa Lewis, we continued to get the insider's take on exploring the Smokies. Wild Bill taught us how to cast a fly rod to catch trout in the mountain streams. We all hiked to Abrams Falls and took a refreshing swim in the stream, in view of a magnificent waterfall. Dad rented tubes and we spent a day lazily floating on the Little River.

Aunt Walks-a-Lot got her wish—we all took an eleven-mile round-trip day hike up to Mt. Le Conte via the Alum Cave Trail. What a spectacular hike it was! The trail followed along Alum Cave Creek, through rhododendron, and up a set of stone steps under a huge arched rock called, quite simply, Arch Rock. We stopped to enjoy a view from Alum Cave, which is really a bluff. Alum Cave served as a mine for Epsom Salts, and was mined for saltpeter during the Civil War. Further up the trail, we had to grip cables placed by the Park Service, to navigate along some precarious cliff edges. On our final approach to the summit we passed through a spruce forest once again, filling our noses with that wonderful Christmas tree fragrance. We stopped at the Le Conte Lodge, a rustic historic mountain lodge with small cabins nestled along the mountainside and a main dining hall. We continued on until we reached the summit marked by a pile of rocks, called a cairn. The stunning views, the bluffs, and dramatic changes in landscape made this my favorite hike of the trip. We all found out why Aunt-Walks-a-Lot was so keen to hike this trail, and I'm glad she insisted we do it with her.

One morning, with Wild Bill and Papa Lewis as guides, we all piled into the vehicles. Next stop: the Metcalf Bottoms picnic area. We parked the vehicles, clipped on our day packs, and took a stroll along the Little Briar Gap Trail. Wild Bill led us along, and after a short walk the trail took us to the Little Green Briar School, remnants of a community long gone.

"This one-room log building served as a school until 1936. Schools like this were scattered throughout the Great Smoky Mountains," Wild Bill explained.

"Why is there a cemetery in front of the school?" Hug-a-Bug asked.

"Too much studying," I joked.

"The school also served as a Baptist Church, which is why there is a cemetery," Papa Lewis explained.

After exploring the grounds, we continued our stroll along the Little Brier Gap Trail to the Walker Sisters Cabin.

"This cabin is the home of some of the last people to live in the park," Wild Bill explained. "Four brothers and seven sisters were raised in this house and six of the sisters lived their entire lives here. After the creation of the park, the Walker sisters sold souvenirs to curious visitors. These women lived off the land until the last one passed away in 1964. Today, many of the original descendants have moved away, but some remain in the area. If an outfitter owner, store clerk, waitress, or park staff that you meet has the same last name as a family that once lived in the park, there's a good chance that person is a descendant."

Our Great Smoky Mountain Adventure was an epic experience. We had crisscrossed this mountainous national park for two whole weeks, and there were still many more adventures awaiting us—but those would have to wait for next time. On our last night in the park, we all sat around a roaring fire, reminiscing about our adventures together. In the morning, we would go our separate ways and these adventures would become dis-tant memories. We all felt tied together by our endless fun in the park. We had shared animal encounters, history, and the raw, natural beauty. It was easy to see why this place had the word "great" in its name. We agreed that we would visit again soon. The Great Smoky Mountains had become a sacred place for all of us.

This trip impressed upon me the importance of main-taining our parks and national wild lands. During our adventure, I felt more energized than I ever had. Papa Lewis explained that I was experiencing the benefits of exercising in the great outdoors and enjoying nature.

I was awestruck that I now had the ability to travel back in time, and the ability to retell stories and bring them to life, like Papa Lewis had done with us, but I was still puzzled as to why our time-travel skills had to be such a secret. I got it that we had to be careful not to alter the past when we time-traveled, so as to preserve history. I understood that people would not believe that I had the ability to go back in time. What I didn't get was why my family had been so secretive about it all these years. Our family mission of preserving our parks and wildlerness is the mission of many volunteers, park staff, wildlife staff, and government agencies. So, why did we have to be so secretive about our mission? Papa Lewis and Wild Bill sat down with Crockett, Hug-a-Bug, and me to talk about it. Papa Lewis started the conversation.

"Someone with devious intentions could alter the entire history of the world if they got ahold of our time-travel skills or time-traveled with us. On top of that, imagine how you might be treated if someone discovered you can time-travel? In the 1600s people who were accused of being witches were executed. I'm not saying that would happen to us, and we're certainly not witches, but we could be taken into government custody or something."

Wild Bill picked up the conversation. "Many in our clan live and work as park staff and volunteers, ready to use their time-travel skills to help in the search for a long-lost plant or animal species. One day we might have to rely on these wild places for our very survival, just like our ancestors did. Our untamed, natural wild lands may hold the key for future generations in discovering new lifesaving medicines. If a plant species is wiped out, perhaps an original specimen could be found in one of our national parks. The clear-cut sections of the Smokies have grown back to forest once again, but several species of trees and plants have not returned. Preservation is key."

Our time-travel secret had brought our family together in a unique way. After our talk with Papa Lewis and Wild Bill, we had a better understanding of the importance of keeping our family time-travel skills a secret, but we still had an unsolved code to decipher. Papa Lewis and Wild Bill weren't aware of any key or code. Crockett, Hug-a-Bug, and I sat looking at the cipher. We placed the two torn halves of paper together under the light of a lantern at the picnic table, hoping to find a clue. I had flipped through the family journal every night since we first pieced the paper together, but I had found nothing resembling a key. Crockett's map, where we had found the other half of the cipher, was unfolded on the table next to us. I had never paid much attention to it before—it was just on older edition of my map of the Smokies. But then I noticed something—printed across Crockett's map in bold letters was 'Great Smoky Mountains National Park.' But the words 'Great National Park' were underlined and someone had added an "s" to park making it 'Parks.' Then it hit me. That same phrase was written in the family journal, on the date that Papa Lewis had received his time-travel skills from his grandfather. We had just discovered the key we needed to break the cipher! The key was Great National Parks.

I shared our discovery with Papa Lewis.

"I bet if you decipher that code, the message will lead you to your next adventure," Papa Lewis said with a smile.

The End.

Bubba Jones'
Great Smoky Mountains
National Park Adventure

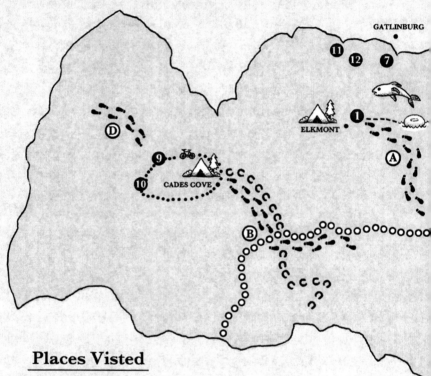

Places Visted

1. Elkmont Historical Area
2. Clingmans Dome
3. Newfound Gap
4. Elk in Cataloochee Valley
5. Cherokee Indian Villiage
6. Oconaluftee Vistior Center
7. Sugarlands Visitor Center
8. Mingus Mill
9. John Oliver Place
10. Cable Mill
11. The Walker Sisters Cabin
12. Little Green Briar School

Activities

O O O Appalachian Trail

 Campgrounds

 Fishing with Wild Bill

 Tubing: Little River Trail

 Bike Tour: Cades Cove Loop

Ɔ Ɔ Ɔ Horse Back Route

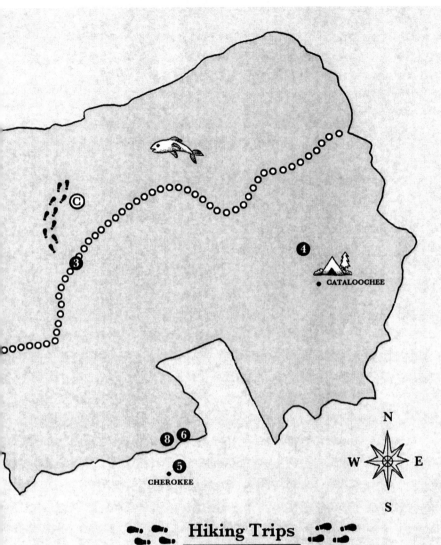

Hiking Trips

(A) Start at Elkmont campground to little river trail- camp at
campsite 24- continue hike up Goshen prong trail end at
Clingmans Dome (one night/ 2 day backpacking trip- one way)

(B) Start at Cades Cove Picnic Area to the Anthony Creek Trail to
the Appalachian Trail-Eagle Creek Trail- camp at Spence Field
Shelter-Eagle Creek Trail to Appalachian Trail to Derrick Knob
Shelter (round trip three day/two night backpacking trip).

(C) Alum Bluff Cave Trail to Mt. LeConte (round trip day hiking).

(D) Abram Falls Trail (round trip day hike)

Curriculum Guide for
The Adventures of Bubba Jones

About the Book

Tommy "Bubba Jones" and his sister Jenny "Hug-a-Bug" learn more about the Great Smoky Mountain National Park than they ever thought they would when Papa Lewis lets them in on a family secret: The family has legendary time traveling skills! With these abilities, Bubba Jones and Hug-a-Bug travel back in time and meet the park's founders, its earliest settlers, native Cherokee Indians, wild animals, extinct creatures, and see what the park was like millions of years ago. With this time traveling ability also comes a family mystery, but the only person who can help solve the mystery is a long lost relative who lives somewhere in the park. Explore the Smokies with Bubba Jones and family in a whole new way. *The Adventures of Bubba Jones* is recommended for grades 3–8 and may be a helpful resource for several curriculum topics listed below.

Social Studies

Native American Indians / Cherokee Indians
Southern Appalachian Culture
Lewis & Clark
Early settlers
Survival
Great Smoky Mountains National Park
Appalachian Trail

Civilian Conservation Corp.

Science
Extinction
Elevation/ Geology
Old-Growth Forest
Secondary Regrowth
Non-native species
Chestnut Blight
Elk
Buffalo
Bear
Synchronized fire flies
Poisonous snakes
Salamanders
A National Park compared to a National Forest

Math
Cipher Code/Problem Solving

The Adventures of Bubba Jones
Discussion Questions

Chapter 1: The Secret Family Legend

1. Who were Lewis and Clark and what are they famous for?

2. What does Bubba Jones's family use their time traveling skills for?

3. Why does Papa Lewis make Bubba and his family take an oath of secrecy? What happened during the T-Rex Incident?

Chapter 2: The Adventure Begins!

1. Name five items on Bubba Jones, Papa Lewis, and Hug-a-Bug's Backpacking Gear List.

2. In this chapter, Bubba Jones and Hug-a-Bug have their first time traveling adventure. What are some of the differences between Elkmont in 1906 and the present day Elkmont campground?

Chapter 3: The Fall of the Giants

1. What is the difference between a national forest and a national park? What might have happened to the Great Smoky Mountains if they had been turned into a national forest?

2. What happened to the American Chestnut Trees?

Chapter 4: The Legend Unfolds With Sparkles in the Night

1. How is a synchronized firefly different than other fireflies?

2. Why did Papa Lewis hand over his powers to Bubba Jones, and not keep them?

3. What are possible consequences of someone else finding out about Bubba's family's time traveling ability?

4. What is a cipher code?

Chapter 5: The Original Great Smoky Mountain Inhabitants

1. What was the Trail of Tears?

2. What was Hug-a-bug afraid that could happen when Bubba got his time travel powers?

Chapter 6: One Big Mountain

1. Why is Bubba able to see a spruce-fir forest at Clingmans Dome? Where do these trees mainly grow?

2. Were the Smokies taller than they are now?

3. At the end of this chapter, Bubba and Hug-a-Bug tell their parents about all of the time traveling adventures they have had so far. If you could travel back in time with them, on which of these adventures would you go? Why?

Chapter 7: Celebrity Sightings at Newfound Gap

1. What is a thru-hiker? Do you think you could thru-hike the way Grandma Gatewood did, or would you need more resources? What else would you bring with you?

2. What were Earl Shaffer and Grandma Gatewood famous for?

DISCUSSION QUESTIONS

Chapter 8: The Other Side of the Mountain

1. What is a trail name and what are some of the trail names that Bubba Jones and his family use?

2. Bubba says that all of his family members have trail names, "based on each one's unique love of adventure and exploring." What would you choose as your own trail name? Why?

Chapter 9: A Big Surprise

1. Name at least three animals that used to call the Great Smoky Mountains home.

2. Why is the elk herd in Cataloochee Valley and not the rest of the park?

Chapter 10: As Real as it Gets

1. What is found at the Oconaluftee Village?

2. Name at least 3 facts about the Cherokee.

Chapter 11: The Wild Goose Chase

1. How does bartering work? What sorts of items were used in bartering? Do you think bartering would still work today? Why or why not?

2. Imagine that you have traveled back with Bubba and his family to Mingus Mill. What sorts of jobs would you have been made to do as a miller back then?

Chapter 12: Away From It All

1. Who were the Olivers? What does Bubba learn about them when he time travels?

2. After seeing how the first Smokies settlers lived in 1825, Bubba's mom says that the settlers "worked so hard just to eat and stay alive." What are some ways that the settlers found food? How did they keep it from spoiling?

173

3. How can you protect yourself from a black bear?

Chapter 13: The Smoky Mountain Biathlon!

1. What is Horace Kephart known for?

Chapter 14: Over the Hills and Through the Woods

1. Where do Appalachian Trail thru-hikers stay while hiking through the Smokies?

2. What makes the wild boar different than most of the other animals living in the Smokies?

Chapter 15: You Can Hike But You Cannot Hide!

1. Why doesn't Wild Bill want to interact with Horace Kephart? What does he think might happen?

2. Where are some of the places Wild Bill visited in the Smokies?

3. What are the names of the two poisonous snakes found in the Great Smoky Mountains?

4. The Smokies is known as Capitol of the World for what species?

5. What did the Civilian Conservation Corp (CCC) do in the Smokies?

Bibliography

United States. Appalachian Trail Conservancy. Accessed February 18, 2015. http://www.appalachiantrail.org/

Alt, Jeff. *A Walk for Sunshine: A 2,160-mile Expedition for Charity on the Appalachian Trail.* New York: Beaufort Books, 2015.

Alt, Jeff. *Get Your Kids Hiking: How to Start Them Young and Keep It Fun.* New York: Beaufort Books, 2013.

"National Park Geologic Resources." NPS: Explore Nature » Geologic Resources » Home. January 28, 2014. Accessed February 14, 2014. http://vulcan.wr.usgs.gov/LivingWith/VolcanicPast/Places/volcanic_past_appalachians.html.

Beard, Bill. *Hiking Trails of the Smokies.* 4th ed. Gatlinburg, Tenn.: Great Smoky Mountains Natural History Association, 1994.

Brewer, Carson, Amanda Summers, and Christina Watkins. *Cades Cove Tour.* Gatlinburg, TN: [Great Smoky Mountains Natural History Association], 2010.

Brewer, Carson. *Day Hikes of the Smokies.* Gatlinburg, Tenn.: Great Smoky Mountains Association, 2002.

Bruchac, Joseph, and Diana Magnuson. *The Trail of Tears.* New York: Random House, 1999.

Cataloochee Auto Tour. Gatlinburg, TN: [Great Smoky Mountains Natural History Association], 1993.

Davis, Frank C. *My C.C.C. Days: Memories of the Civilian Conservation Corps.* Boone, N.C.: Parkway Publishers, 2006.

Dunn, Durwood. *Cades Cove the Life and Death of a Southern Appalachian Community, 1818-1937.* Knoxville: University of Tennessee Press, 1988.

Dykeman, Wilma, and Jim Stokely. *Mountain Home: A Pictorial History of Great Smoky Mountains National Park.* Gaitlinburg, TN: Great Smoky Mountains Association, 2008.

Edgar, Kevin. *Appalachian Trail Guide to Tennessee-North Carolina.* 11th ed. Harpers Ferry, W. Va.: Appalachian Trail Conference, 1995.

BIBLIOGRAPHY

Ellison, George. "A Look Back at Kephart's Cabin." April 27, 2011. Accessed December 23, 2014. http://www.smokymountainnews.com/news/item/3857-a-look-back-at-kephart's-cabin?t.

Ellison, George. "Where the Buffalo Roam." Where the Buffalo Roam. November 10, 2010. Accessed November 15, 2014. http://www.smokymountainnews.com/news/item/2478-where-the-buffalo-roam.

Fisher, Noel C. *The Civil War in the Smokies*. Gatlinburg, Tenn.: Great Smoky Mountains Association, 2005.

Frazier, Ian. "Hogs Wild." The New Yorker. December 12, 2005. Accessed December 20, 2014. http://www.newyorker.com/magazine/2005/12/12/hogs-wild.

Frome, Michael. *Strangers in High Places*. Expanded ed. University of Tennessee Press, 1980.

Great Smoky Mountains National Park Official Junior Ranger Program Booklet. Gaitlinburg, Tenn: Great Smoky Mountains Association, 2007.

Great Smoky Mountains National Park: Return of the Elk. Gaitlinburg, Tenn: Great Smoky Mountains Association, 2013.

Great Smoky Mountains National Park: Synchronous Fireflies in the Smokies. Gaitlinburg, Tenn: Great Smoky Mountains Association, 2013.

Gugliotta, Guy. "A Major T. Rex Breakthrough: Broken Bone Leads to Discovery of Soft Tissue." The Washington Post. March 25, 2005.

"Online Exhibit: Hall Cabin." Horace Kephart: Revealing an Enigma. January 1, 2005. Accessed December 14, 2014. http://www.wcu.edu/library/DigitalCollections/Kephart/onlineexhibit/HallCabin/index.htm.

Houk, Rose. *Smoky Mountain Elk*. Gaitlinburg, Tenn: Great Smoky Mountain Association, 2013.

Jolly, Harley E. *The CCC in the Smokies*. Gaitlinburg, Tenn: Great Smoky Mountains Association, 2001.

Kephart, Horace. *Our Southern Highlanders*. New York: Outing Publishing Company, 1913.

Kephart, Horace. *Smoky Mountain Magic: A Novel*. Gaitlinburg, Tenn: Great Smoky Mountain Association, 2009.

Kephart, Horace. *The Cherokees of the Smoky Mountains*. Gaitlinburg, Tenn: Great Smoky Mountains Association, 1936.

Koontz, Katy. *Family Fun in the Smokies*. Gaitlinburg, Tenn: Great Smoky Mountain Association, 2012.

LaFevre, John and Kat. *Scavenger Hiking Adventures: Great Smoky Mountains National Park*. Guilford, Conn: The Globe Pequot Press, 2007.

McMahan, Carroll. "Millionaire's Row at Elkmont Offered Idyllic Summer Respite." Upland Chronicle. March 25, 2014.

BIBLIOGRAPHY

Accessed November 20, 2014. http://www.thegreatsmokies.net/ millionaires-row-elkmont-offered-idyllic-summer-respite/.

Manning, Russ, and Sondra Jamieson. *The Best of the Great Smoky Mountains National Park: A Hiker's Guide to Trails and Attractions*. Norris, Tenn.: Mountain Laurel Place, 1991.

Morgan, Emily R. *Next Time You See a Firefly*. Arlington, Va.: National Science Teachers Association, 2013.

Mussulman, Joseph. "Jefferson's Cipher for Lewis." Jefferson's Cipher for Lewis. June 5, 2006. Accessed January 29, 2014. http://www.lewis-clark. org/content/content-article.asp?ArticleID=2222.

United States. National Park Service. "Great Smoky Mountains National Park (U.S. National Park Service)." National Parks Service. Accessed April 25, 2014 & February 18, 2015. http://www.nps.gov/grsm/index.htm.

Peters, Gerhard, and John T. Wooley. Franklin D. Roosevelt: "Address at Dedication of Great Smoky Mountains National Park.," September 2, 1940. The American Presidency Project. Accessed February 18, 2015. http:// www.presidency.ucsb.edu/ws/?pid=16002.

When Mama Was the Doctor: Medicine Women of the Smokies. Smoky Mountain Publishers, 2010. DVD.

t, Dave. "Cades Cove CCC Camp." Cades Cove CCC Camp. January 13, 2005. Accessed December 14, 2014. http://cadescovepreservationtn.home-stead.com/cadescoveccccamp.html.

Priestly, Kent. "Light and Shadow: The Mystery and Legacy of George Masa." Mountain Xpress. August 26, 2009. Accessed December 18, 2014. https:// mountainx.com/arts/art-news/082609light_and_shadow/.

Rockwell, Craig. "The Secret Code of Lewis and Clark." The Secret Code of Lewis and Clark. Accessed January 14, 2014. http://www.lewisandclarktrail. com/legacy/secretcode.htm.

Roll, Kempton H. "THE SOUTHERN APPALACHIAN MOUNTAINS." The Southern Appalachian Mountains. Accessed January 1, 2014. http:// main.nc.us/sams/blueridge.html.

Shaffer, Earl V. *Walking With Spring: The First Solo Thru-Hike of the Legendary Appalachian Trail*. Harpers Ferry, WV: Appalachian Trail Conference, 1995.

Shields, Randolph. *The Cades Cove Story*. Gaitlinburg, Tenn: Great Smoky Mountains Association, 1981.

Schmidt, Ronald G. and William S. Hooks. *Whistle Over the Mountain: Timber Track & Trails in the Tennessee Smokies*. Yellow Springs, OH: Graphicom Press, 1994.

Urie, Michael, and Randall Kremer. "Dinosaur Discoveries in Montana: T. Rex and Triceratops Go to Smithsonian and Museum of the Rockies." Smithsonian Museum of Natural History. August 20, 2002. Accessed January 1, 2014. http://www.mnh.si.edu/press_office/releases/2002/montana.pdf.

BIBLIOGRAPHY

Tabler, Dave. "A Town Dies, a Park Is Born - Appalachian History." Appalachian History. August 16, 2012. Accessed October 9, 2014. http://www.appalachianhistory.net/2012/08/today-former-town-of-elkmont-tn-in.html.

"Walker Sisters Cabin." The Great Smokies. Accessed December 27, 2014. http://www.thegreatsmokies.net/walker-sisters-cabin.

Weals, Vic. Last Train to Elkmont: A Look Back at Life on Little River in the Great Smoky Mountains. Knoxville, Tenn: Olden Press, 1993.

Non-Publication sources:

Dietzer, Bill. Lecture, January, 2015.

Ezell, David. Lecture, Townsend, TN, October, 2014.

Museum of the Cherokee Indian, Cherokee, North Carolina. October 2014.

Oconaluftee Indian Village, Cherokee, North Carolina. October 2014.

Soehn, Dana, e-mail correspondence, Management Assistant / Public Affairs, The Great Smoky Mountains National Park. February, 2015.

Tennessee State Library and Archives (Nashville), Dept. of Conservation Photograph Collection.

ABOUT THE AUTHOR

Jeff Alt is an award-winning author, a talented speaker, and a family hiking and camping expert. Alt has been hiking since his youth. In addition to writing *The Adventures of Bubba Jones* book series, Alt is the author of *Four Boots—One Journey*, *Get Your Kids Hiking*, and *A Walk for Sunshine*. *A Walk for Sunshine* won the Gold in the 2009 Book of the Year awards sponsored by Fore Word Reviews; it took first place winner in the 2009 National Best Books Awards Sponsored by USA Book News, and won a Bronze in the 2010 Living Now Book Awards sponsored by Jenkins Group. *Get Your Kids Hiking* won the bronze in both the 2014 Living Now Book Awards and the 2013 IndieFab Awards in Family and Relationships. Alt is a member of the Outdoor Writers Association of America (OWAA). He has walked the Appalachian Trail, the John Muir Trail with his wife, and he carried his 21-month old daughter across a path of Ireland. Alt's son was on the Appalachian Trail at six weeks of age. Alt lives with his wife and two kids in Cincinnati, Ohio.

For more information about *The Adventures of Bubba Jones* visit: www.bubbajones.com. For more information about Jeff Alt visit: www.jeffalt.com.

E-mail the author: jeff@jeffalt.com.

CPSIA information can be obtained at www.ICGtesting.com
Printed in the USA
LVOW10s0402180615

442912LV00001B/1/P